Catherine Cook   as born at Tyne
Dock, part of the Tyneside scene she
re-creates so vividly in her novels, and
most of her early years were spent in
what was then the small hamlet of
East Jarrow. After leaving school she
followed a variety of occupations,
finally moving south to Hastings
where she met and married a local
schoolmaster, and has lived there ever
since. Over the years she has
established herself as one of the most
popular of the contemporary English
regional novelists.

and published by CORGI BOOKS

Mary Ann and Bill

Catherine Cookson

CORGI BOOKS
A DIVISION OF TRANSWORLD PUBLISHERS LTD

MARY ANN AND BILL

A CORGI BOOK 0 552 09397 1

Originally published in Great Britain
by Macdonald & Co. (Publishers) Ltd.

PRINTING HISTORY

Macdonald edition published 1967
Corgi edition published 1974

This book is set in Plantin 10/11 pt.

Corgi Books are published by Transworld Publishers Ltd.,
Cavendish House, 57–59 Uxbridge Road, Ealing,
London, W.5.

Made and printed in Great Britain by
Richard Clay (The Chaucer Press), Ltd., Bungay, Suffolk.

Dedication
To Foster and Rose Mary.
A generation does not
divide us.

CONTENTS

CHAPTER ONE

WORDS

Mary Ann sat in the living-room above the garage and looked at her children, and she wondered, and not for the first time, why it was possible that you could be driven almost demented by those you loved most; if it wasn't Corny, it was one of the twins driving her to the point where she wanted to break things.

When the great stroke of luck had befallen them a few months earlier she had thought that all was set fair now for peace, plenty and pleasure. She couldn't have been more mistaken.

Peace, with that noise going on across the road! What had once been fields overlaid by a wide canopy of sky that she could look into from the bedroom window, was now a contorted mass of scaffolding and buildings in the process of erection. Even to the side of the house, on the spare bit of land, there was hammering and battering and clanking going on all hours of the day; and whereas, at one time, they were lucky to get half-a-dozen customers for petrol during the day, now the custom was so thick they never seemed to close.

This white elephant of a garage, off the beaten track from the main road, which they had supported for seven years in the hope that the road would be extended to take them in had never materialised. Instead, Mr. Blenkinsop, the American, had. And Mr. Blenkinsop had transformed Green Lane and Boyle's garage into a place where the last thing one expected now was peace.

As for plenty, Corny had always said that when his ship came in he'd build her a fine house on this very spot, or anywhere else she liked; they'd get a spanking new car; they'd take a holiday, not a fortnight, but a month, and abroad, and it would be first-class for them from beginning to end; no mediocre boarding-houses for Mrs. Mary Ann Boyle. These were the things he had promised her just before he went to sleep at nights, and she forgot about them the next day, knowing they were but dreams. Yet when the miracle happened and he could have built them a house, bought a smashing car, especially as he was in the business, and taken them for a holiday, what had happened? He couldn't leave the garage; he had to be here at Mr. Blenkinsop's beck and call. As for the house, that would have to wait; let Mr. Blenkinsop get the factory up first and let him get the garage premises extended on the spare land, and then he would think about a house. As for the holiday, well, she could take a week off if she liked, but he couldn't come along.... So much for plenty.

And pleasure? Oh! pleasure. She had never had less pleasure in her life than during these last few months. Corny was so tired when he came upstairs he couldn't even look at the television. As for going out, say to Newcastle, to the pictures, even that was a thing of the past since the miracle had happened.

All she seemed to do now was to cook more because there was always somebody popping in for lunch. Mr. Blenkinsop and his cousin Dan from Doncaster, who was now in charge of the works, and other big pots who were interested in the new factory. She had liked doing it at first because she liked being told she was a smashing cook, but she found you could weary of praise when a mountain of dishes kept you going well into the afternoon; and a box of chocolates and a bunch of flowers failed to soothe you since they couldn't wipe up.

And besides the peace, plenty and pleasure, there were the twins. She had always considered she could manage the twins. Even during all those long years when David hadn't been able to speak and his dumbness made him obstinate she had been able to cope with him, but since he had begun to talk six months ago she had found him almost unmanageable. He would lapse into long aggravating silences, during which no one could get a word out of him; but when he did talk the substance of his conversation was such as to make you wonder how on earth he had come by his knowledge, and sometimes create in you a desire to brain him for his precociousness, and at other times to laugh until you cried at his patter.

But this evening she felt no way inclined to laugh at her small son. Anyway, he was in one of his obstinate moods and she could also say that so was she herself. She was fed up to the teeth with this day and all its happenings; from early morning she had been on the go. She had made arrangements to go and get her hair done when Corny had phoned up to say that Mr. Dan Blenkinsop had just come in from Doncaster; how about a cuppa? And she had made a cuppa, and over it Mr. Blenkinsop had been so talkative and charming that the time had gone by and now it was too late for her to keep her appointment in Felling, and her hair looked like nothing on earth, and Corny had accepted the invitation of Mr. Blenkinsop for them all to go to Doncaster tomorrow.... Well, she wasn't going. She would just tell Corny and he could phone and call it off; she wasn't going looking a mess like this. In any case it was he who accepted the invitation and not her. He had jumped at it like a schoolboy, saying, 'Oh, that'll be grand, a day out. And the twins will be over the moon to see the boys.'

She had memories of the last time the twins and Mr. Daniel Blenkinsop's four sons had met. Neither the house nor the garage had returned to order for a week afterwards.

But in the meantime she would use the promised trip—about which their father had already informed them—as a means of making the children come clean regarding why David had been kept in at school.

'You tell me what he's been up to, Rose Mary, or there'll be no trip to Doncaster tomorrow for anybody.'

Rose Mary lowered her eyes from her mother's face and slid them towards her brother, but David had his gaze fixed intently on the mantelpiece and, because it meant he had to look over the top of his mother's head, his chin was up and out, and Rose Mary knew from experience it was a bad sign. Their David never talked when he pushed his chin out, no matter what he was looking at. There was a vague yearning in the back of her mind for the time past when their David couldn't

11

talk at all. Everything had been lovely then. She had looked after him and talked for him, and he yelled if he couldn't be with her, but now the tables were turned so completely that he yelled if she insisted on being with him. The only thing their David wanted to do now was to muck about with cars, and get all greased up. He didn't play any more. She didn't see why she kept sticking up for him, she didn't. But when she saw her mother's hand jerk forward suddenly and grip David by the shoulders and heard her voice angry sounding as she cried, 'Don't put on that defiant air with me! I warn you, you'll go straight to bed. That's after you get a jolly good smacked backside,' she shouted as loudly, 'Aw, Mam, don't. Don't bray him. He'll tell you.'

Rose Mary was hanging on to her mother's arm now, and, her lips trembling and her voice full of tears, she looked at her brother and cried, 'Well, tell her you! If you don't I will, 'cos I'm not goin' to not go to Doncaster the morrow through you. See! 'Cos you won't play with me if we don't go, so tell her.'

Both Mary Ann and Rose Mary now concentrated their gaze on David; and David stared back into his mother's eyes and remained mute, and Mary Ann had her work cut out not to box his ears instantly.

Aiming to keep in command of the situation, Mary Ann turned her eyes slowly away from her son's penetrating stare and, looking at her daughter, said, 'Well, it's up to you.'

Rose Mary swallowed; then, her head drooping on to her chest, she whispered, 'He swore.'

'SWORE!' Mary Ann again looked at her son. 'You swore? Who did you swear at?'

Rose Mary once more supplied the information. 'At Miss Plum.'

'You didn't, David; you didn't swear at Miss Plum!' Mary Ann was really shocked.

David's round face stretched slightly as he pulled his lower lip downwards and pushed his arched eyebrows towards the rim of his ginger hair.

'What did you say?' Mary Ann's voice was tight, and when the only response she got was the further pulling down of his lip and the further pushing up of his eyebrows she put the question to Rose Mary, 'What did he say?'

Rose Mary blinked, then bit on the nail of her middle finger before she said, 'Lots.'

'Lots! You mean he swore more than once?'

'Ah-ha.'

Mary Ann closed her eyes for a moment. She knew this would happen some time or another. The boy spent too much time down in that garage and with the workmen on the site, and knowing some of the adjectives used by the workmen, she trembled to think which one of them he had levelled at his teacher.

'Go on, tell me,' she said. She addressed her daughter.

Rose Mary nipped at her lower lip; then, wagging her head from side to side, she cast a glance at her brother, who was now staring straight at her, and said, 'Fumblegillgoozle.'

'Fumble-gill-...? But that's not a word. I mean, that's not swearing.'

The twins now exchanged a deep look which Mary Ann could not interpret, and she said, 'Well, it isn't. It's a made-up word, isn't it?'

'Yes. Yes, Mam; but Miss Plum said that he said it like swearin'.'

Mary Ann hadn't a doubt but that her son could put the inflection on fumble-gill-goozle to make it sound like swearing. He was learning words, he was fascinated by words, and he had a way with his inflection. 'Is that all he said?'

'No, Mam.' Again the brother and sister exchanged a deep glance before Rose Mary, continuing with the betrayal, whispered, 'Antimacassar.'

Again Mary Ann closed her eyes, this time to prevent herself from laughing outright. When she opened them she looked directly at her son and said, 'Antimacassar and fumblegillgoozle aren't swear words. But it all depends how you use them, and you know that, don't you, dear?'

'Yes, Mam.' It was the first time he had spoken since he had come into the house, and the sound of his own voice was like an ice breaker cleaving a way through his imposed silence, for now he added rapidly, 'I don't like Miss Plum, Mam. She's

13

big. And I don't like her hands. And when she bends over you you can see right down her throat, and she'd had onions. And she marked me sums wrong and they weren't wrong; and she gave Tony Gibbs ten, and he's a fool. Tony Gibbs is a fool. An I told her I'm not sittin' next to her at mass on Sunday any more. I told her I'm goin' to sit with Rose Mary....'

'Yes, yes, he did, Mam. He told Miss Plum that.'

Rose Mary's face was alight with her pleasure. For many months now she had been deprived of her twin's company in so many ways, and to be separated from him in church was to her the last straw. It had been Miss Plum's idea to keep them apart, hoping that the separation might go some way towards enabling David to break the dominance of his sister. Undoubtedly this strategy had helped towards David's independence, but now there was nobody more aware than David that he did not need Miss Plum's help, or that of anyone else for that matter, to make him talk.

'You cheeked Miss Plum, David?'

'No, no, I just told her.'

'You must have cheeked her.' Mary Ann was bending towards him. 'What else did you say?'

David looked up into his mother's face. His eyes were twinkling now, and the corner of his mouth was moving up into a quirk, when Rose Mary spluttered, he spluttered too, until Mary Ann said sharply, 'Stop it! Stop it, the both of you. Now I want to know what else you said.'

They stopped their giggling and David lapsed into his silence again and Rose Mary said, '...Gordon Bennett, Mam, and Blimey Riley.'

Mary Ann swallowed deeply. Gordon Bennett was a saying that Jimmy down below in the garage often resorted to. He didn't swear much in front of the children but his intonation when he said 'Gordon Bennett!' spoke volumes. And Blimey Riley. Well, that was one Corny often came out with when he was exasperated. He would exclaim between gritted teeth 'Bl-i-mey, Riley!' and it certainly sounded more like swearing than swearing. So, in a way, David had sworn.

Poor Miss Plum; she had her sympathy. She had thirty-eight in her class and she needed only two or three Davids to

14

drive her round the bend. She said now sternly, 'Miss Plum had every right to keep you in, and if I had been her I would have given you the ruler across your knuckles.' She looked from one straight face to the other. 'And don't think you're out of the wood yet. Wait till I tell your father about this. Now go and get yourselves washed and then come back and have your tea. And there's no play for you until I say so, understand?'

They stared at her for a moment longer, then as if governed by the same impulse they turned together and went out of the room, and as they passed through the door she cried after them, 'What is that you said, David?'

She was on the landing now looking down at her son. She took him by the shoulders again and shook him. 'Tell me what you said.'

When she paused for a moment and his head stopped bobbing, he spluttered, 'Rub-rubber guts.'

Mary Ann drew in a deep breath that seemed to swell her small body to twice its size, and she twisted him round and grabbed him by the collar and thrust him into the bedroom to the accompanying pleas of Rose Mary, crying, 'Oh, no, Mam! Oh, no! Don't, don't Mam. Don't bray him.'

With one hand she thrust Rose Mary back on to the landing, then, standing with her back to the bedroom door, she swiftly stripped down David's short pants and laid the imprint of her hand four times across his buttocks. And then she released him and, panting, stood looking down at him.

She was looking now not at a cheeky little devil, but at a little boy with the tears squeezing from under his tightly closed lids, and she had the desire to grab him up into her arms and soothe him and pet him and say, 'There, there! I'm sorry, darling, I'm sorry.' But no; Master David had to be taught a lesson. Rubber guts, indeed!

When she turned and hurried from the room she almost fell over Rose Mary, and she yelled at her, 'Get into that bathroom and get yourself washed! You're as bad as he is. Wait till your father comes in. There's going to be a change in this house; you see if there isn't.'

'Oh, Mam, Mam, you shouldn't; you shouldn't have hit our David. I'll tell me da of you. I will. I will.'

15

Now Rose Mary found herself lifted by the collar and thrust into the bathroom and her dress whipped up and her knickers whipped down, and she screamed open murder as Mary Ann's hand contacted her rounded buttocks. And when it was over she sat on the floor and looked up at Mary Ann and cried between her gasping, 'I don't love you. I don't love you. I'm going away. I'm going away to Gran's. And I'll take our David with me. I will, I will. I don't love you.'

Mary Ann went out, banging the bathroom door after her; and on the landing once more she put her hand up and cupped her face. 'I don't love you. I don't love you.' The words were like a knife going into her. Although she knew it was a momentary spasm, and one she had indulged in many a time herself, it had the power to send her spirits into the depths.

She was just going into the kitchen when Corny came bounding up the stairs. 'What's the matter? I could hear her screaming downstairs. What's up?'

Mary Ann sat down on a chair and looked up at her tall, homely-looking red-haired husband, and what she said was, 'Oh, Corny!'

Dropping on to his hunkers, Corny gathered her hands into his and gazed into her twisted face as he asked softly, 'What is it, love? What's the matter? What's happened?'

'I . . . I don't know whether to laugh or cry. I . . . I think I'll cry. . . . I've . . . I've had to skelp both their behinds.'

'Well, it won't be the first time. But what's it about, anyway?'

'He's . . . he's had one of his defiant moods on. They were kept in at school. He's been swearing at Miss Plum.'

'No!' He sat back on his hunkers; then grinned, 'Swearing? What did he say?'

'Antimacassar.' She watched him droop his head on to his chest, and when his eyes, wide and merry, came up to meet hers, she said, 'And fumblegillgoozle.'

'. . . Fumble-what?'

'That's what I said, fumble-what. It's one he's made up. Fumble-gill-goozle. Have you ever heard anything like it?' He shook his head.

'But that isn't the worst. . . . Gordon Bennett.'

16

'Oh, no!'

'Yes, Gordon Bennett. And you can imagine the emphasis he would put on it. And wait for it, Mr. Boyle.' She inclined her head towards him. 'Blimey, Riley!'

He took one of his hands from hers and covered his mouth to smother his laughter; then his shoulders began to shake.

'And he called me rubber guts.'

The next minute his arms were around her and their heads were together.

After a moment she pressed herself away from him and, looking into his face, she said, 'We can laugh, but, you know, it's serious. He's got this thing about words; you never know what he's coming out with next. And I've told you he spends far too much time down in the garage, and on the site, and you can't put a gag in men's mouths.'

'Well, he doesn't hear anything really bad down in the garage. There's only Jimmy there; he might come out with a damn and an occasional bloody.'

'It's plenty.'

'Aw.' He rose to his feet. 'If he hears nothing worse than that he won't come to much harm.'

'He does hear worse than that on the site.'

'Well, I can't tie him up, and I can't keep my eye on him all the time, we've just got to let things take their course. He's a lad, Mary Ann. You see'—he turned to her again—'all his life, not being able to talk, he was cut off. To him it must feel as if he'd been born just six months ago, and from the minute he found his voice, he's been experimenting. Let him be and don't worry. Come on, up you get.' He pulled her to her feet, then ended, 'It's a break you need. Tomorrow's a day out; it'll do you good.'

She looked up at him, saying coolly, 'A day out you said? Who for? The Blenkinsop boys?'

'Oh, it won't be a repeat of the time they were here. There's plenty of room up their place. That big field beyond. And then there's the ponies and what not. Once you get there you won't see them or ours until we're coming back. I've got a feeling it's going to be a good day.... Come on, let me inject you with that feeling, Mrs. Boyle.' Swiftly he picked her up in his arms

17

and kissed her hard, and when he put her down again he said, 'There, how's that? Feel the difference?' And when she replied, 'Not that you'd notice,' he said, 'You know, the trouble with you, Mrs. Boyle, is you're growing old.'

She didn't laugh with him or retaliate in any way but, going into the scullery to start the tea, she thought, 'Yes, I am growing old. I'm twenty-seven.' And the train of thought caught a grievance that was in her mind a lot of late, that asked her what had she done with her life? What was she doing with her life? The answer came as before, nothing, except cooking and cleaning, and washing and shopping, and worrying, and waiting for Corny to come up from the garage so she would have company; then watching him going to sleep watching the telly. Then awakening to it all over again the following morning.

Yes; she was twenty-seven, and she was getting old.

CHAPTER TWO

THE DAY OUT

Rose Mary looked up unsmiling into her mother's face. Although she loved her mother again this morning she wasn't really kind with her, because she hadn't said she was sorry about braying them last night.

They had an arrangement regarding clearing the air after incidents like last night. Whoever was at fault was to be the one to say sorry, and then everybody was kind again. There was no doubt in Rose Mary's mind that her mam was at fault for braying them, because, she reasoned, Miss Plum had punished David for swearing, or for sounding like swearing, and it was awful for her mam to lather into him again.

When Mary Ann said, 'Now, let either of you get a mark on your clothes and you're for it. Do you hear me?' she said stiffly, 'Yes, Mam.'

'Do you hear me, David?'

'... Yes, Mam.'

'Well, remember it. Now go downstairs, but don't you move away from the garage drive. And don't go into the garage. Understand?'

They both looked at her silently, then turned and walked slowly away.

The scene outside was most unusually quiet today. There were no cranes and grabs clanking across the road; no sound of men's voices shouting; no lorries churning up the mud in the lane; and for once no car standing at the petrol tanks opposite the wide space that led into the hangar-like shed that constituted the workshop and garage.

Bringing her eyes to David, who was standing with his hands thrust deep into his pockets, Rose Mary now said, 'She never said she was sorry.'

He returned her glance and wagged his head twice before saying, 'I don't care.'

'Neither do I.'

'I know some more words.' He slanted his eyes at her.

'Eeh! our David. You'd better not. Mam'll give it to you.... What are they?' She leant her head towards him, and he grinned at her, then whispered 'Skinnymalink.'

'Oh, that's not a word; I know that one.'

He jerked his head; then said, 'Well, you don't know skilligalee.'

'Eeh! skilligalee.' She whispered the word back at him. 'Where did you get it?'

'One of the men.' His chin was jerking again.

'Is it a bad swear?'

'Ah-ha.'

'Eeh! our David. Mam'll tan you purple if she hears it.'

He grinned at her again, then walked jauntily towards the opening of the garage, and Rose Mary followed him. And there they both stopped and looked into the dim interior where Jimmy was standing talking to a shock-haired, tight-trousered young man, whom they recognised as Poodle-Patter, the nickname given to one of the group with which Jimmy played.

As David went to move forward Rose Mary pulled him back, saying, 'Don't go in; Mam'll be down in a minute, and you know what she said.'

'I'm not going in; I'm just going to the office door.'

'Eeh! our David.' Rose Mary remained where she was, but David moved forward, and at the office door he stopped and cocked his ear to hear Jimmy say, 'Yes, I know I could get more money at Baxter's but I don't want to go, man.'

'You must be barmy.' Poodle-Patter dug Jimmy in the chest with his fist. 'Five quid a week more and you're turning your nose up at it.'

'I'm not turning me nose up at it, man. It's just that I'm well set here. I'm all right.'

'How long is it since you had a rise?'

'Couple of months since.'

'How much?'

'Ten bob.'

'Ten bob!' Poodle-Patter's nose crinkled in scorn. Then leaning towards Jimmy, he said, 'You want to come in with us in the car, don't you?'

'You know I do.'

'Well then you'll have to do something about it. Duke's got his eye on this mini-bus. He can get it for two hundred if we put the money down flat, I told you, but if it's spread over it'll mean another thirty quid on it, and as Duke says somebody's got to take the responsibility of the never-never and he's not going to. He's been done afore, you remember? It's cash and equal shares: forty quid each, then we'll all have a say in it.'

'Forty quid?' Jimmy's voice was scornful. 'I couldn't raise forty shillings at the minute, and you know it. Look here, Poodle.' He now dug his finger into Poodle's chest. 'You an' Duke an' the rest talkin' about responsibilities, well, I've got responsibilities; and to me mam. There's only one wage comin' into our house, and that's mine; and there's three of us to keep on it, with Theresa still at school. You can tell Duke from me he can buy his blasted car and count me out.'

'Ah, don't get ratty, man; you know we wouldn't do anything without you. Anyway, you're necessary to our lot and we know it; there's not one of us knows owt about a car, we'd have to pay God knows what for repairs. You've kept The Duchess going over the last year when she should have been on the scrap heap. I don't know how you've done it. I said so to Dave and Barny. "I don't know how Jimmy does it," I said. Look.' Poodle-Patter moved nearer to Jimmy, his voice wheedling now, 'I'm not asking you to do anything out of line, I'm only saying make a move. Everybody should make a move, and you've been in this dump long enough. And it isn't as if you're not sure of a job. I tell you, Baxter's are wantin' somebody like you, a bloke with experience. And that's the basic they're paying, fifteen quid a week. Will you think on it?'

'Look!' Jimmy bowed his head while thrusting his fist out towards Poodle, and Poodle, playfully gripping it between his hands, wagged it, saying, 'That's a boy! That's a boy! Sleep on it. There's no real hurry, not really; The Duchess has carried us a good many trips, she'll carry us a few more. I'll tell Duke you're considering it. Look, I must be off. See you, fellow.'

Poodle now punched Jimmy once more in the chest, then turned swiftly towards the garage opening, and when he passed Rose Mary he put his hand out and chucked her chin, saying, 'O-o-oh! hello there, gorgeous.'

Rose Mary blinked her eyes and tossed her head. She wasn't displeased with the title of gorgeous. All Jimmy's band called her gorgeous, but Jimmy didn't because he knew her dad wouldn't have let him.

As she saw David move further into the garage she whispered hoarsely, 'No, our David! Mam'll be down in a second; you'll only get wrong.'

David didn't appear to hear her, for he walked towards Jimmy, who was now standing with his two hands on the bonnet of a car, his head bent forward as if he was thinking deeply, and he looked up at him for some seconds before he said, 'Jimmy.'

'Oh; hello there.' Jimmy straightened himself up, then grinned down at the small boy. 'By, you look smashin'. I never knew you looked like that; it must be 'cos you've been washed.'

David did not grin back at his friend but considered him seriously for a moment before saying, 'You wouldn't leave here, would you, Jimmy?'

'Leave here? ... Aw.' Jimmy jerked his chin to the side. Then looking down slantwise at David, he said, 'Trust you to hear things you shouldn't. You've got lugs on you like a cuddy.'

'But you wouldn't, would you, Jimmy?'

'No.'

'But you'd get five pounds more at Baxter's.'

'Aye, I'd get five pounds more at Baxter's, so what?'

'Why ... why don't you ask Dad for more money?'

'Look.' Jimmy dropped on to his hunkers and, his face level with David's, he was about to put his hands on his shoulders when he stopped himself and exclaimed, 'Eeh! I just need to do that and I'll have your man knock the daylights out of me.'

22

He rubbed the palms of his oily hands together and said, slowly now, 'Your dad gave me a rise just a while ago. That's the second in six months, and who knows, maybe I'll get another one shortly. I'm satisfied, so what is there to worry about?'

David stared unblinkingly into the long, kindly face. Although Jimmy neither came upstairs for meals nor slept in their house he considered him part of his family; he liked him next to his mam and dad. He didn't place Rose Mary in his list of affections; because Rose Mary was already inside of him, part of himself. He might fight with her, tease her and torment her, but he also listened to her and considered her views and demands as if they were issuing from his own brain. He asked now quietly, 'Will they put you out of the band if you don't help to buy the car?'

Jimmy put his head on one side and began to chuckle; then he shook it slowly before he said, 'You know, you're a rum customer. You know what I think? I think you've been here afore. Me mother always says that some folks have been here afore. She says that they couldn't know what to do at an early age unless they had learned it in another life.' He drooped his head to the other side, adding. 'You don't know what I'm on about do you? But to answer your question. Aye, very likely if I don't fork out they might. . . .'

At this moment there came the toot-toot of a motor-horn and Jimmy, stretching his long length upwards, exclaimed, as he smiled at David, 'Ah, here we go again,' then went out towards the petrol pumps and the customer.

David was once more standing beside Rose Mary when Mary Ann and Corny appeared on the drive. He watched his father walk slowly towards Jimmy, then stand waiting while Jimmy took the money from the driver, saying, 'A pound and sixpence.'

The man in the car handing Jimmy two pound notes, said, 'I'm sorry I haven't any less,' and Jimmy replied 'That's all right, Sir, I'll get you the change.'

Within seconds he came back from the office and, looking at Corny, said, 'I haven't got it in the till; can you change it, boss?'

'No, not a pound note,' said Corny, then bending towards the man in the car, he said, 'We'll call it straight.' He nodded towards Jimmy, and Jimmy handed the man the pound note back again.

'That's very kind of you.' The driver smiled up at Corny, saying, 'I'll have to remember to call this way when I'm coming back and do the same again.'

They all laughed now.

As the car drove away Mary Ann said to no one in particular, 'That's the third time to my knowledge you've run out of change in a fortnight. Oh! Oh!' She raised her hand, 'It's only sixpence I know. It was only threepence before, and a shilling before that. But what's a shilling? And what's sixpence? And what's threepence in a fortnight? Only one and nine. But there's fifty-two weeks in a year. Cut those by half, and you have twenty-six one and ninepences. At least.' She turned round now and confronted both Corny and Jimmy.

There was a grin on Jimmy's face but he remained silent.

There was a grin on Corny's face too, and he said airily, 'Yes, twenty-six one and ninepences up the flue. . . . But, Mrs. Boyle.' He walked towards her, then took her arm and led her into the garage towards their car. 'Did you hear what that gentleman said? I'll call this way when I'm coming back. Now. He's no fool, and he knows I'm no fool; I'm not going to do that every time he calls in. But the impression is made, the good impression. He'll tell his friends. He won't say they'll get cheaper petrol here, or that this garage bloke doesn't care about money; he'll say, "Go to Boyle's, you'll get service. It's a good garage." Aw, to heck!' He pulled open the car door. 'What does it matter? We needn't worry about the coppers any longer. Get yourself in, woman.' He slapped at her bottom. 'Aren't I always telling you "them days are gone"? Come on you two.' He yanked the children into the back of the car, and as he started her up he said in grave, dignified tones, 'Remember, Mrs. Boyle, you're married to a man with a bank balance that is getting blacker and blacker every week. Twenty-six one and ninepences. . . . Rabbit feed!'

When she dug him in the ribs he laughed; then pushing his head out of the window, he called to Jimmy, saying, 'Now, you'll lock up at six and see everything's O.K. before you leave ... right?'

'Don't you worry, boss. Have a nice time.'

And Mary Ann called, 'And don't forget to turn the gas off. I've left it in the oven for you, a pie; it just needs warming. Half-an-hour.'

'Right-o, Mrs. Boyle. Thanks. Thanks. ... Bye-bye, nippers.' He waved to the children, and they waved to him.

As the car swung into the road Mary Ann sat back and sighed. It was nice after all to get away for a day, away from the honk-honks, the smell of petrol and the irritations, which were still present even when the banging and noise had ceased. She sighed again. She would enjoy today. Yes, she would enjoy today. And it went without saying that the twins would; they loved the Blenkinsop horde. She was about to turn to them when the unusual quiet that prevailed in the back of the car was forced on her notice and she nipped at her lips to suppress her smile. The events of last night were evidently still with them and they were expecting her to say she was sorry. Well, they could expect. Rubber guts, indeed!

Corny, too, noticing the absence of chatter remarked under his breath, 'No talkie-talkie from backie-backie' and she replied softly and in the same idiom, 'Coventry. Waiting for sorry-sorry, but no feely like it.'

When Rose Mary saw her mam and dad laughing quietly together she felt slightly peeved; she hadn't been able to make out what they were talking about. She wanted to lean over and say, 'What you laughing at, Mam?' She always liked to be in on a joke. But she wasn't kind with her mam. Yet she was still kind with her dad, so she could talk to him.

She leaned towards Corny now and said, 'Do you know Annabel Morton, Dad?'

'Annabel Morton? No.' His head went up as if he was thinking. 'Never heard of her in me life.'

'Oh, Dad!' Rose Mary pushed him in the back. 'You do know Annabel Morton. I'm always talking about Annabel Morton. She's a beast, and she's Miss Plum's favourite. You do know Annabel Morton.'

'Oh ... h! that Annabel Morton. Oh yes, I know that

stinker. She's dreadful; she's terrible; she's horrible; she's. . . .'

'Dad! you're takin' the micky.'

'Oh, no, I'm not; I'm just agreeing with all you've said about that Annabel Morton. What's she done now ... that Annabel Morton?'

'Well, yesterday dinner-time, after we came out of the hall, Patricia Gibbs was telling me about the girl who lives next door to her and who's going to be married in a long white dress with a train, and a wreath and veil and everything, and she's going to marry a priest.'

Mary Ann's head, on the point of jerking round, stopped abruptly and she continued to gaze ahead while she waited and left the sorting of this one to Corny.

'Oh, she's going to marry a priest, is she? Is she a Catholic?'

'No; she said she wasn't, but she's going to marry a priest.'

'It'll be a minister she's going to marry.'

'No, no, I said that, 'cos I know they're called ministers, and misters, but she said no, he was a priest and she was going to marry him.'

'Oh, I think she made a mistake,' said Corny. 'It wouldn't be——'

'It wasn't a mistake, Dad. And as we were talkin' about it Annabel Morton had her lugs cocked and she said Patricia Gibbs was barmy and she'd picked a barmy one to tell it to, and she meant me, and I slapped her face for her.'

After a short pause Corny said, 'In a way, I think Annabel Morton was right this time. I think Patricia Gibbs is a bit barmy if she says that the girl is going to marry a priest.'

There was another short silence before Rose Mary said, 'Well, why can't priests marry, Dad?'

Corny was saved from trying to explain a situation that was beyond his understanding by his son saying, ' 'Cos they can't marry people, women, you nit, they can only marry nuns.'

The car seemed to do a side-step. In the middle of a splutter Mary Ann cried, 'Careful!' Then with her head down she said, 'Look where you're going.'

'They don't marry nuns. Eeh! our David. Nuns can't marry; they're angels.'

There was a short silence now as David tried to digest this. Then he put the question to his father's back. 'They're not, Dad, are they? Nuns aren't angels. They've got legs, haven't they?'

The car took another erratic course before Corny replied thickly, 'Well, angels could have legs....Speaking of legs——' Corny now aimed to direct the conversation into safer channels. 'Did you bring your football boots?'

'No, Dad.'

'Well, you won't have any toes left in your shoes when Brian and Rex get that ball going.'

'Do you think we'll see Susan and Diana?' asked Rose Mary now.

'Perhaps,' said Corny. 'We'll see Susan, anyway.'

'Well, we didn't last time; she was away on the comple-ment.'

'Continent.'

'Yes, Dad; that's what I said, complement.'

Another short pause before Rose Mary stated, 'I like Susan; she's nice. She said I'm going to be tall like you, Dad. I want to be tall, I don't want to be little.'

'Stabbed in the back.' Mary Ann muttered the words below her breath, and Corny muttered back, 'Better give in and get it over.'

'Susan says when you're tall you can....'

Mary Ann turned around and surveyed her offspring, look-ing first at Rose Mary, then at David, then back to Rose Mary again. She said quietly, 'I'm sorry.'

Rose Mary wriggled her bottom on the seat, drew her lower lip right into her mouth, drooped her head, then wagged it from side to side before raising it sideways and glancing at David.

David's reactions had not been so obvious. All he did was to sit on his hands and lower his lids.

Then, again as if released by one spring, they were standing up and their arms were about Mary Ann's neck and they were laughing as they cried, 'Oh, Mam! Mam!'

'There now. There now. You'll choke me. Sit down. Sit down.'

27

David sat back on the seat, but Rose Mary lingered. Her mouth rubbing against Mary Ann's ear, she whispered, 'I was only having you on, Mam. I don't care how big I am.'

Mary Ann kissed the face so like her own; and when she was settled in her seat again she looked at Corny, whose amused glance flashed to hers, and she thought, as she had done often as a child, It's going to be a lovely day, beautiful.

The Dan Blenkinsops lived in an old house on the outskirts of Doncaster. It had the added attraction of a tennis court, a paddock and a strip of woodland.

Dan and Ida Blenkinsop had six children, four boys and two girls. Tommy, the youngest, was eight; Rex was ten; Brian, eleven; and Roland, thirteen; then there was Susan, fifteen, and Diana, nineteen.

Mary Ann had met all the family with the exception of Diana, and she was looking forward to meeting Mr. Blenkinsop's eldest daughter, for she would likely see a great deal of her in the future as she was going to act as secretary to her father who was now in the position of managing director of the English side of Blenkinsop's Packing Company.

Mary Ann was now sitting in the corner of a luxurious couch which was upholstered in pale blue satin and bore the imprint of grubby hands and, even worse, dirty feet. She looked about her at the lovely pieces of furniture, all, to her mind, ill-treated; cups and glasses standing on the grand piano; a conglomeration of boys' implements, all of a destructive nature ranging from catapults to guns, and including a bow and arrow, lay piled on what was evidently an antique desk. The Chinese carpet showed the tread of dirty shoes all over it, and from where she sat she could see into the hall and to the bottom of the stairs where a long coloured scarf hung like a limp flag from the banisters. She could see shoes lying jumbled on the parquet floor, and coats and sweaters heaped on a chair.

Mary Ann smiled to herself. It took all sorts to make a world. And in this world of the Blenkinsops there was evidently no discipline but a lot of fun. Also, she sensed there was a lot of money squandered needlessly. Yet, she had to admit, the children didn't act spoilt. They were very good-mannered and charming—that's when they were forced to stand, or to sit still for a moment, but most of the time they seemed to be bounding, jumping or rushing somewhere, yelling, shouting and calling as they went. And their mother wasn't in the least affected by it.

Mary Ann now watched Mrs. Blenkinsop come into the room. She never seemed to hurry. She was tall and rather graceful, with black hair and black eyes, in sharp contrast to her husband who was very fair, and, incidentally, much shorter than his wife.

Mrs. Blenkinsop came straight towards Mary Ann, saying, 'Diana's coming; you've got to pin her down when you can.' She sank on to the couch, adding, 'She's making the best of the time left to her. She loves riding; she's never stopped all the holidays. Ah.' She turned her face towards Mary Ann, 'But they're only young once, aren't they?'

She was speaking as if to an equal, and quite suddenly Mary Ann again felt old, like she had done last night. Mrs. Blenkinsop must be forty if she was a day, but her words seemed to imply that they were both of a similar age and frivolity was past them.

Mr. Blenkinsop now came across the room, walking with Corny. He was saying, 'Well, the main office is ready and that's all that matters at present. Get the brain working and the body will take care of itself.' He laughed his hearty laugh, adding, 'Anyway, from Monday next that'll be my head-quarters and. . . .' He paused and looked towards the door and, his voice rising, he added, 'And that of my able secretary, Miss Diana Blenkinsop.'

From the very first sight of the tall, leggy, blonde-headed, extremely modern-looking Diana, Mary Ann experienced a feeling of apprehension, even danger, for there arose in her immediately the fighting protective feeling that she had lived with, and acted on, during the years of her childhood . . . and after. The feeling had centred then around her father, but now it wasn't her father who was bringing it to the fore, but her husband.

She looked at Corny standing in front of the girl who was

29

almost his height, and his ordinary looking face, which at times appeared handsome to her, was, she imagined, looking its most attractive at this moment. The girl, she noted, had almond-shaped, wide-spaced blue eyes and she was using them unblinkingly on Corny. It wasn't until her father drew her attention away by saying, 'And this is Mrs. Boyle,' that she turned from him.

Mary Ann didn't stand up. She was at a disadvantage sitting down, but she knew she would be dwarfed still further if she got to her feet.

'This is Diana. Now you two will be bumping into each other pretty often, I'm sure, so the sooner you get acquainted the better.'

Diana lowered herself down on to the arm of the couch, and Mary Ann was forced to put her head well back to look up at her, and she made herself speak pleasantly to the disdainful-looking madam, as she had already dubbed her.

'Will this be your first post as secretary?'

'No.' The voice was cool, matching the whole appearance. 'I've been with Kent, the solicitor, for three months. . . .'

'Oh, and then she was with Broadbent's.' It was her mother speaking now. 'She was there for nearly six months, weren't you, dear?' It was as if Mrs. Blenkinsop was emphasising that her daughter wasn't without experience.

'You're going to find it a change from a solicitor's.' They all looked at Corny. He was seated opposite the couch and he was looking directly at Diana Blenkinsop, and she looked back at him as she asked pointedly, 'What way, different?'

'Oh.' He jerked his head. 'Well, a bit rougher, I should say. There are nearly two hundred chaps knocking around there and you'll be the only female. Oh, of course, except Mary Ann.' He now looked towards Mary Ann, and she looked back at him. Oh of course, except Mary Ann, he had said. She wasn't a female; she was just some gender that passed unnoticed among two hundred men.

'Oh, we're not worried about Diana.' Mrs. Blenkinsop was walking towards the french windows. 'She can take care of herself.' She cast a smiling glance back to her daughter before going on to the terrace and calling, 'Roland. Brian. Lunch.

Bring them in . . . lunch.'

Mr. Blenkinsop now seated himself beside Mary Ann and began to talk to her. She had a feeling that he was trying to be kind, going out of his way to be kind. When she looked at him she thought he was in much the same position as herself, being small. Perhaps he was being kind because he knew what it felt like to be confronted by the big types, either male or female.

His effort was checked by the avalanche of his four boys and their sister, Susan, together with her own two. They all came into the room yelling at the top of their voices; even Rose Mary and David. She wanted to check them but resisted. And then Rose Mary had hold of her hands, gabbling, 'Oh, Mam! Mam, you must come and see them. They're beautiful, lovely, aren't they, David?'

'Oh yes. Come and see them, Mam, will you, 'cos they're super.'

She smiled her bewilderment not only from one to the other, but also to the group of Blenkinsops, who were all around the couch now, and they explained in a chorus, 'The puppies. . . . The Grip's had puppies.'

Fancy calling a dog, a female dog, The Grip; yet she remembered her one and only encounter with the family's bull terrier, and the name, she imagined, wasn't entirely inappropriate, although they had assured her The Grip was as gentle as a kitten . . . with people. With other dogs it was a different matter, they explained. Apparently, she had earned her title from her power to hang on to any four-footed creature which earned her dislike. But now The Grip had had puppies. It was odd that anything so fierce was capable of motherhood. Mary Ann widened her eyes and showed pleased surprise and assured them that she would love to see The Grip's puppies.

'But not before lunch,' said Mrs. Blenkinsop emphatically, as she shooed the children into the hall, with orders to wash.

A few minutes later they were all in the dining-room, and Mary Ann was both impressed and saddened by the quality of the silver and china used, and the chips and cracks in the latter. And she was almost horrified at the toe and heel indentations on the legs of the period table and chairs. It was all right being free and easy, she thought, but the condition of this beautiful furniture almost amounted to vandalism. But, as her dad was always saying, it took all kinds.

The lunch, she considered, was very ordinary, and the food would have been completely dull if it hadn't been enlivened with wine. She took note that Corny allowed his glass to be filled up three times, and also that the two Blenkinsop girls and Roland were allowed wine, and the boy was only thirteen. By the end of the lunch she told herself this was an entirely different way of living from her own; nevertheless, she preferred her own every time.

The children's demands that they should go to see the puppies cut short any lingering over coffee, and Mary Ann wasn't displeased that they should get outside, because she was finding herself irritated by Diana Blenkinsop's supercilious attitude, and more so because it seemed lost on Corny, for he was talking to her as if he had known her all his life; and she had even condescended to laugh at something he said.

But one thing Mary Ann told herself as she walked down the garden by Mr. Blenkinsop's side, nodding politely as he talked without really paying much attention to what he was saying, was that when they left here she must say nothing detrimental about Diana Blenkinsop. She must keep her spleen to herself; all the books told you that you got off on the wrong foot when you showed your jealousy. Not that she was jealous. Oh no; it was only that Corny had seemingly found Diana Blenkinsop attractive, and if she should voice the opposite view about her it would only show her less attractive by comparison. . . . That's what all the books said.

They came to the paddock and the stables, and here, in a wire-netting enclosure, were The Grip and her six offspring.

The barking and yapping of the young puppies was overlaid by the exclamations of admiration from the children.

Mr. Blenkinsop stooped down and picked up one of the puppies and, putting it into Rose Mary's arms, said, 'There. What does he feel like?'

'Oh, Mam! Mam!' Rose Mary was laughing hysterically as she strained her face away from the puppy's tongue and endeavoured to hang on to his wriggling body.

'She may drop it,' said Mary Ann anxiously, and Mr. Blenkinsop said, 'It's all right, I've got him. But she mustn't drop this one because he's the prize pup. Thirty-five guineas' worth there. He goes tomorrow.'

'Thirty-five guineas!' Corny was making appreciative movements with his head.

'Yes. It seems a lot,' said Mr. Blenkinsop, 'but she's a thoroughbred. And what's more, I'm going to be out of pocket by the time they all go. You have no idea ... I'm telling you you've no idea what it takes to feed these youngsters. But, thank goodness, they'll all be gone by the end of the month, with the exception of Bill there.' He pointed to where David was scratching the tummy of one of the pups who was lying on its back. 'He's the runt.'

'What's the matter with him?' Mary Ann asked politely.

'Oh, nothing really, except that his chest is too broad. It's supposed to be broad—these brindles are noted for their chests, but they've got to have legs to support them, like this one here.' He took the puppy from Rose Mary's arms and held it up. 'You see, his front legs are as straight as broom shanks, but when Bill there grows, his weight will make him bandy. But he's full of life. He's a lad, is Bill.'

'Dad!' Amid the hubbub David's voice went unheard. 'Dad! Dad!' He tugged at his father's sleeve.

'Yes, what is it?' Corny bent over David, and David looked up into his father's eyes, then down at the puppy lying on its back. 'Aw-w! I don't know about that.' Corny straightened up; then looked at Mary Ann and said under his breath, 'He's after a pup.'

Mary Ann gave him one telling look. A pup indeed! she had enough to put up with without a dog going mad round the house. Oh, no! She was about to turn away in the hope of drawing her offspring with her when David's voice hit her, crying loudly, 'Mam! Mam!' And she looked down at him and said under her breath, 'No, David.'

But Rose Mary had picked up the scent now. Standing close to Mary Ann she caressed her hand and looked up at her pleadingly, saying, 'Couldn't we, Mam? Couldn't we?'

'No! And that's final. And stop it.' Mary Ann was hissing now.

It would seem that Mr. Blenkinsop had not heard any of the exchanges, at least he gave a good imitation of being unaware of what was going on, for, stooping down, he picked up the now bounding puppy and, bringing it over the wire, held it in front of Mary Ann and said, engagingly, 'Can I make you a present of him?'

'WH ... !' Mary Ann swallowed, blinked her eyes, glanced wildly around her, then was forced to take the puppy into her arms, and her acceptance or refusal was drowned by the shrieks of delight from both Rose Mary and David, and these were echoed by the entire male side of the Blenkinsop family.

'Oh good. I'm glad you're going to have Bill,' cried Roland; and Brian, endorsing his brother's words, said, 'We wondered what would happen to him. We wouldn't be able to keep him, you see, not with The Grip. Sort of mother and son, you know.'

And so Mary Ann, who didn't want a dog, who had never really been fond of dogs, well, not since she was a child, who felt herself cramped and restricted in the confines of her four small rooms, and whose life at the moment seemed full of drudgery and empty of anything creative, was now to be saddled with a dog, and, of all breeds, a bull terrier, which type was known for its ferocity. She'd go mad. And this, without taking into account the future, in which Diana Blenkinsop portended to move large. But with eleven people all milling around, all expounding in different ways on Bill's virtues, what could you do but just smile. She was still smiling when Diana, staring her straight in the face, said, 'Runts are always unpredictable, but the best of luck.' Whereupon, Mary Ann had an almost uncontrollable desire to reach up and slap her face. Eeh! she'd be glad when she was home.

It was a quarter to one when Corny was roused from a deep sleep by a small hand on his face and a voice whispering, 'Dad! Dad!'

'Yes ... yes. What is it?'

'It's Bill, Dad. He's howling. He's crying.'

'Look, Rose Mary!' Corny too was whispering hoarsely now. 'Go on back to bed.'

'But he misses his mam, Dad. And it's the first night. Could we not bring him up ... ?'

'No! Definitely no. Get back to bed.'

'But, Dad.'

'Look. Do you want your backside skelped? Go on; you'll wake your mam, and David.'

'David's awake, Dad; he's on the landing, top of the stairs.'

'Oh my God!' The words were muttered thickly as Corny dragged himself out of bed, and, pushing Rose Mary before him, he groped his way out of the dark room and on to the darker landing.

'David!'

'Yes, Dad.'

'Get yourself back into bed this instant.'

There was no movement from the head of the stairs.

'Do you hear me?' Corny felt his son groping his way across the landing; then he followed him into the small room and switched on the light, and, looking from one to the other, he said, 'Bill's not coming upstairs. That was agreed last night. Now, wasn't it? He's got to sleep downstairs. You know what your mother said; you were lucky that she brought him. Now don't press your luck, and get back into bed, both of you!'

The last three words were like the crack of a whip. With a lift of his hand he hoisted David into the upper bunk, and without another word he switched off the light and groped his way back into his own room again.

Corny hadn't slept side by side with Mary Ann for eight years not to know when she was asleep or awake, even if she was silent. As he wriggled himself down under the clothes he said, 'Don't say it,' and for answer she replied very quietly, 'I'm going to say it. You evaded the issue when we came to bed by very conveniently going straight to sleep, but I saw you giving Mr. Blenkinsop the wink to pass the puppy on to me. You wanted that dog as much as they did, and you saw the only way to get it was to put me on the spot. Well now, you got your way and what are you going to do about it? Just listen to him.'

For a moment they lay and listened to the heart-rending

35

howls that came up through the floor boards from the garage where Bill was ensconced in a blanket-lined wash-basket. Corny, making no reference to the duplicity of which he was accused, grunted, 'He'll get used to it.'

'But what are we going to do until he does? He's been like that for the last two hours.'

'You've been awake all that time?' He turned quickly and drew her into his arms, where she lay unyielding against him.

'I'm sorry, love; I'm sorry. But ... but they wanted him. Yes, yes, I know I did an' all. I've always wanted a dog about the place, and he's cute. You'll get to like him. He's cute.' He squeezed her.

'O-o-o-o! Ow'll! Wow! Wow! WO-OW-OOO!'

'Oh my God!' Corny pulled the clothes over their heads, and as Mary Ann pushed them back again she remarked coolly, 'You'll get used to it.'

'Now, look; don't take that attitude. Very likely I will get used to it. I'll have to, won't I? But don't be snooty and so damn self-righteous.'

Corny turned round on to his other side again and again put his head under the bedclothes. . . .

At half-past-two, dragging on his trousers with such ferocity that he pulled off the brace belt, he went from the room and down the stairs and, unlocking the garage, grabbed up the yapping pup and marched upstairs with it to the kitchen where, dragging a cushion from a chair, he put it inside the fender, near the oven, and plonked the now quiet animal into the middle of it. Bending down close to it, he growled, 'Now, another word out of you, just one more peep, and out of the window you go.'

Bill stared up at Corny with his small round eyes, then he opened his mouth and yawned widely. He understood. The first round had been won.

Mary Ann arose at half past six. She didn't always get up so early, and after the night she'd had she needed extra rest, but something told her that she should rise. Perhaps it was the small scufflings from behind the wall to the right of her.

When she entered the kitchen she stopped dead, absolutely

dead, and so did Bill.

Bill was in the middle of disembowelling the armchair; he was covered all over with kapok, and he gave two delicate sneezes to rid his nose of the fluff adhering to it; then he jumped down from the chair and bounded towards her. Mary Ann let him jump around her feet as she leant against the door, with one hand on the knob and the other across her mouth. Inside the fender was the remains of a cushion; on the hearth rug was what had once been a tea towel; the woollen hand-knitted tea-cosy that she had bought from the bazaar just a few weeks ago had almost returned to its original state of unknitted wool. Great lengths of it stretched from one corner of the room to the other, and the legs of a chair had taken on the appearance of a loom. All that was left of the tea cosy was the pink woollen rose that had adorned the top. And pervading this chaos was a peculiar smell. It was what her da had been wont to call a widdle scent. He had said that animals didn't smell, they just gave off a widdle scent.

Widdle scent! Three puddles and two mounds of dark matter, the result, no doubt, of the extra mince with which the children had fed him.

'Get away!' Her voice was almost a thin scream. She slapped her hand so hard on his rump that he was bowled over sideways. But Bill was a friendly, forgiving chap, and he showed it by again jumping up at her. For this show of affection he found himself being lifted by the scruff of the neck and thrown into the scullery and the door banged on him. Well, well; that's what a fellow got for simply passing the time until people turned up.

Mary Ann now stalked into the bedroom, and when she ripped the bedclothes from her husband he sat bolt upright, spluttering, 'W ... what.... What is it? what's the matter?'

'Would you mind coming into the kitchen.'

'Aw, Lord!' Corny flopped back on to the bed again. 'He's wet. All right, he's wet. I'll wipe it up.'

'Corny!'

He opened his eyes, there was a danger signal in that note. He got out of the bed and followed Mary Ann out of the room and into the kitchen. There he took one look then closed his eyes tightly and muttered deeply and thickly, 'Oh, Christopher Columbus!'

When he opened his eyes again she was standing a yard from him, the tears glazing her cheeks, and he went to her and said softly, 'I'm sorry, love, I'm sorry. I'll keep him downstairs. I promise.'

'Have . . . have you seen the chair?'

He looked towards the disembowelled chair. Then drooping his head, he said, 'I'll get you another. This very day, I'll get you another, a better one.'

'It's . . . it's one of a pair. It's spoilt the pair.' Her whole face was trembling.

'I'll get you a pair. It doesn't matter about that, but . . . but I'll kill him for this, see if I don't. Where is he?'

Corny would have had to be deaf not to know where Bill was, and he made for the scullery door, only to stop before opening it and say, 'I'd better get my things on first.'

A few minutes later, carrying Bill by the scruff of the neck, he took him downstairs and thrust him into the basket in the garage, and, holding him there, he addressed him. 'Look here. The quicker you learn to put up with this the better for all concerned. This is your home. Now understand that, this basket, this place.' He beat the side of the basket with his hand and rolled his head to indicate the garage.

Bill, sitting on his hindquarters, now thrust out the tip of a very pink tongue, and, lifting his right front paw, he wagged it at Corny, and Corny rubbing his hand across his brow, said, 'Aw, man, it's no use; you won't last a week at this rate, she won't put up with it. And I don't blame her. Look, if I'd had any idea of what you were going to do upstairs you could have yelled your lungs out; and you will the night.'

The paw was still flapping at him, and after raising his eyes heavenwards and shaking his head he took it and said, 'All right, all right. But I'm warning you. You've got to stay mum if you want to last out here.'

CHAPTER THREE

LIKE MOTHER LIKE DAUGHTER

This was the third time Rose Mary had been to confession. She had been frightened the first time, but she wasn't any more. Father Carey was nice, but she wouldn't like to go to Father Doughty. Eeh! no. They said he gave you awful penances like standing on your head and walking on glass in your bare feet, but Father Carey just said, 'Say one Our Father and three Hail Mary's.' She liked Father Carey. She was trying to explain to him now a particular kind of sin; the sin of telling her mother she didn't love her while all the time she loved her a lot, heaps and heaps.

'Why do you keep telling your mother you don't love her?' The priest's voice was very soothing.

' 'Cos of Bill.'

'Bill?'

'Our dog.'

'OO-h!'

'Mam says we've got to get rid of him.'

'She doesn't like Bill?'

'No; 'cos he tore up the chair and the tea-towels, and he howls all night, and he makes widdles and dollops all over the place if he's let upstairs.'

The priest cleared his throat and it was some seconds before he was able to say, 'Well, you must train your dog.'

'He doesn't want to be trained, Father; he jumps all over you and licks you. He's nice, Father.'

There was another silence before the priest said, 'What kind of a dog is he?'

'He's a bull terrier, Father.' Rose Mary thought the priest groaned. 'Father.' She craned her face up to the dark mesh that separated her from the faint outline of the hand that was cupping the youthful cheek of Father Carey. 'Will you pray that she'll like him, Father, make something happen sort of that she'll like him?'

The hand moved on the face and she could see the mouth now, the lips moving one over the other; then the priest said, 'You want a miracle.'

Rose Mary's eyebrows, stretching upwards, seemed to make her grow taller because she was now seeing Father Carey's whole head as she exclaimed on a high note, 'Oh yes, please, Father. Oh yes! that would do it, a miracle.'

The priest's voice was hurried now and slightly stern and very dampening as he said, 'You've got to pray awfully hard for miracles, awfully hard; they're not easily come by; you've got to work at them. What you'll have to do is to be very good and please your mother and keep the dog out of her way for a time while you train it.'

'Yes, Father.' Her voice was meek but some part of her mind was answering him in a different tone altogether, saying, 'Ah, man, we've done all that.'

'Now, for your penance say one "Our Father" and three "Hail Mary's", and be a good girl.'

It was dismissal, but she knelt on; and then she said, 'But I haven't said me act of contrition, Father.'

Her eyebrows again moved upwards because she thought she heard the priest saying, 'Oh, lord!' Like that, like their David said sometimes, not holy-like at all.

'Make a good act of contrition.'

'Oh, my God, I am very sorry that I have sinned against Thee because Thou art so good and by the help of Thy Holy Grace I'll never sin again. In the name of the Father, Son-HolyGhostAmen. Ta-rah, Father.'

'Good night, my child.' The priest was coughing badly now.

She left the confessional with her head bowed, her hands joined, and she acted holy all the way to the rail of Our Lady's altar. And there she said her penance; and there, very much as her mother had done not so many years ago, she laid her problems before the Holy Family, and not only the problem of the

40

dog, but the problem that was really, in a way, more important.

She would like to have told Father Carey about this other problem but it was a jumbled confused mass of impressions in her mind; there was nothing clear cut about it as there was about Bill. Bill either went or he stayed; yet this other problem, in a way, was also about going and staying, and it concerned her mam and dad and ... her. She always thought of Diana Blenkinsop as her. She didn't like Diana Blenkinsop, and this troubled her too because she liked all the other Blenkinsops, all the boys and Susan, and Mr. Blenkinsop and Mrs.... Well, she liked Mrs. Blenkinsop a little bit, not a lot, but she hated Diana, 'cos Diana made her da laugh, and that made her mam angry, proper angry.

Diana Blenkinsop was always coming to the garage for this and that. She hadn't seen her herself because she was at school, but she had heard her mam asking her dad at night why she had to leave her office so often. She had asked did Diana want her dad to sharpen her pencils for her. That could have been funny but it wasn't; it was sort of frightening. And now, even when she tried to explain this problem to Our Lady, who was holding Jesus and looking down on her, she found she couldn't formulate her fears into words; all she could say was, 'Please, Holy Mary, will you make me mam happy again and laughin' like, like she was a while back.'

David was waiting for her outside of the church. He was kicking his toecaps alternately against the kerb. She said to him immediately, 'Did you ask him to do something about Bill?'

He looked sideways at her before drooping his head; then he replied briefly, 'No.'

'Oh, our David ... you!' She walked away, and he followed her, just a step behind, and she said over her shoulder, 'You're no help, are you? Yet what will you do if she won't let us keep him?' She slowed her step and they walked together now, glancing at each other.

'Father Carey says we want a miracle. He's going to try.'

'Don't be daft.'

'I'm not daft, our David. That's what he said. But he said

41

we'll have to work at it.'

'How?'

She shrugged her shoulders. 'Train Bill.'

'Train Bill!' he repeated scornfully; then added, 'You know what Dad said.'

Yes, she knew what her dad had said: anybody who could train Bill would qualify for a lion tamer. Not that Bill was like a lion, he was just playful, slap-happy like. She said now, 'I hope he hasn't yapped all day.'

'Some hope.'

'You're some help, our David.' Her voice was high. 'You do nothing about anything, never.'

'I do so.'

They were standing confronting each other in the middle of the street now. 'I do something about lots of things you don't know about.'

'Like what?'

'Never you mind.'

'Tuppence you don't fight.' They turned their heads quickly and looked at the man who was passing them with a broad grin on his face, and they both walked away, Rose Mary remarking, 'Cheeky thing.'

They were unusually quiet on the bus journey home, but it wasn't their nice conductor so there were no remarks made, and once they got off at the end of the road they ran all the way up the lane.

This time last year the lane had been bordered by hedges; now there was no hedge on the left side and the area appeared to be a moving mass of men and machinery. Just before they reached the white stones that edged the garage drive the buzzer went and all around them became black with men hurrying towards cars and motor-bikes.

They both ran into the garage, as they always did, to say 'Hello!' to Corny and to see how Bill was faring, but tonight their steps were checked at the entrance, for there stood their dad leaning nonchalantly against the side of a car talking to Diana Blenkinsop. They were looking at each other and smiling, and Rose Mary turned away as Corny put his head back and laughed; then she turned quickly back again as she realised there was no excited yapping or bounding body tripping them up. David must have sensed this at the same time because he called loudly to Corny, saying, 'Dad! Dad! where's Bill?'

'Oh.' Corny straightened his back; then pointing, he said, 'He's out the back in the woodshed; he's been under my feet and nearly driven me mad.' He jerked his head in the direction of the far end of the garage.

The children stared at him for a moment, then transferred their gaze to Diana Blenkinsop, and she, looking down at them, said, 'Hello there. Had a nice day?'

When neither of them answered, Corny said, 'You're being spoken to. Miss Blenkinsop was asking you a question.' His voice and face were stiff.

'Yes,' said Rose Mary.

'Yes,' said David. Then together they walked away down the garage.

'Hello there, nippers.' They both turned their heads in the direction of a car that was standing over the repair well, and they called back to the figure squatting underneath, 'Hello, Jimmy, we're going to see Bill.'

'Oh, Bill. Coo! he's been a devil the day.'

They said nothing to this but went through the small door that led on to open ground and across it to the shed.

Bill's whining faded away as they unlatched the door, and then they were almost smothered with shavings.

'Oh, Bill! Bill!' Rose Mary turned her face away from the licking tongue and David, falling back on to his heels, cried, 'Hold it! Hold it!' Then, oblivious of the dirt, they were both kneeling on the floor, holding the dog between them, and Bill quivered his pleasure from his nose to the extreme tip of his tail.

When eventually they got to their feet and ran back to the garage Bill was bounding between them, barking joyously now. As they neared the small door David stopped and, grabbing at Bill's collar, said, 'You go and ask Mam for a piece for me and I'll take him down into the field.'

Rose Mary's face puckered. This wasn't fair; yet it would be more unfair to take Bill back into the garage and have him getting wrong, so she cried, 'Well, don't go far away mind, 'cos if you do I won't bring you any. Just the first field.'

He was running from her now, with Bill at his heels, and Rose Mary, too, ran into the garage. But once through the door she stopped, for her mother was in the garage. She was standing some yards away from her father and Diana Blenkinsop, but Diana was talking to her. She was smiling as she said, 'It's patience that's needed. You've got to have a way with animals, they need handling. With some you've got to take a firm hand. I think Bill's one of the latter.'

There was a slight pause before Mary Ann said, in a voice that sounded cool and thin to Rose Mary, 'And he's not the only one.'

There was a funny silence in the garage now and all of a sudden her mother turned towards her, as if she had known all the time she was there, and grabbing her hand, took her through the small door again, across the open ground and through the gate into their back yard, and she never let loose of her hand until they reached the landing. Then quite suddenly she stopped and leant against the wall and put her two hands over her face.

'Oh, Mam. Mam.' Rose Mary had her arms around her waist now. 'Don't cry. Oh, don't cry. Please, please, Mam.'

Mary Ann stumbled blindly into the kitchen and, sitting down in the armchair, turned her face into the corner of it.

'Oh, Mam.' Rose Mary was stroking her hair. 'I hate Diana Blenkinsop, I do, I do. I hope she dies. I'll scratch her face for her so I will.'

Mary Ann raised her head, her eyes still closed, and she gulped in her throat a number of times before she said, 'Be quiet. Be quiet.' She did not say, 'How do you know I'm crying because of Diana Blenkinsop?' This was her child, flesh of her flesh, brain of her brain. She herself hadn't to be told when, as a child, she had watched her mother suffer.

She was about to get to her feet when the sound of Corny's quick heavy tread came to them, and she muttered under her breath, 'Go on out to play; don't hang around. Do you hear? Go out to play.'

Rose Mary was going out of the kitchen as her father burst

in. He banged the door behind him and stood against it and he looked to where Mary Ann was taking the table-cloth from the sideboard drawer. It was some seconds before he spoke, and this alone was evidence of his anger.

'Now look, we've got to have this out.'

Mary Ann spread the cloth over the table, stroking down the edges, then turned to the sideboard again to get the cutlery. And now he was standing behind her. 'Listen to me.' When his hand came on her shoulder and he swung her round she sprang from him, her face dark with anger as she cried, 'Yes, I'll listen to you. But what are you going to tell me; that I've got a vivid imagination? That it's all in my mind?'

'You insulted her.'

'WHAT! I INSULTED HER! ... All right then, I insulted her. Now perhaps it'll get through that thick skin of hers that it isn't a done thing to throw herself at a married man.'

'Aw, don't be so ridiculous, woman.'

'Ridiculous am I? She's been down below—' she thumbed the floor—'She's been down below three times today to my knowledge.'

'Her father sent her. He wanted some papers, consumption of petrol. . . .'

'Consumption, me grannie's aunt! Every day last week she was in the garage. Every time I went down I saw her there. Consumption of petrol! Papers! Huh! They've got a phone attached from the main office to yours, haven't they? Look, Corny.' Her voice suddenly dropped. 'You're no fool, and you know I'm no fool. If this had been happening to somebody else you'd say that girl wants a kick in the backside, that's what you'd say. You would say she's taking advantage of her father's position; you'd say she's a supercilious big-headed madam. And there's something else you would say. You would say she's sex mad.'

Corny's face was a dull red—it seemed to have caught alight from his hair—and his voice had a blustering note as he answered, 'All right, all right. Say she's all that, say you've hit the nail on the head, now what about me? It takes two to make a deal. What kind of a fool do you take me for?'

45

'A big one.' Her voice was quiet and bitter. 'Somebody's going to get hurt before this play is over and it won't be Miss Diana Blenkinsop. You'll be just one of the male heads she's cracked in passing. She's out for scalps. She's the same type as her mother; I can imagine the same thing happening years ago....'

'Aw, for God's sake!' He put his hand up to his brow. 'It's Mrs. Blenkinsop now.'

'No, it isn't Mrs. Blenkinsop now. We'll stick to her daughter; that's quite enough to be going on with.'

They were staring at each other in bitter, painful silence. Then Corny, his head moving in small jerks and his body seeming to slump, said quietly, 'Ah, Mary Ann, what's happened? Look.' He moved a step nearer to her. 'You know how I feel. God in Heaven, woman, there's never been anybody in my life but you. You know in your heart all this is bunkum; there's only you for me, ever ... ever.'

She gulped in her throat but her eyes held his steadily as she said, 'Yes, I know there's only me for you; and you know I'm safely tucked away in these four small rooms, cooking, cleaning, washing, looking after the children. I'm for you up here, but downstairs you're having your fun. All right, all right.' She lifted her head. 'It could be innocent on your side, but I know girls, and I'm telling you, that girl is in deadly earnest. And in your heart of hearts you know it too.'

She drew in a deep breath now before adding, 'We've talked about this in the past, haven't we, about men going off on the side and coming back and being forgiven? And women doing the same thing. And we've agreed that neither of us could tolerate that; neither of us could take back the soiled article, because that's what it is. The old-fashioned term of the woman being soiled still held good for us.' She moved away from him back to the sideboard, and from there she said, 'It's up to you.'

His body seemed on the point of exploding with the rising tide of anger as he stalked to the door, and from there he turned and bawled at her, 'Aye, it's up to me! And I'm not going to jeopardise all I've worked for to pander to your jealous whims. If you had any blooming sense, woman, you would

46

realise that although Mr. Rodney Blenkinsop put me on my feet I've still got to depend on Dan Blenkinsop. He could just as easily contract with Riley's on the other side of the field for his petrol, or Baxter's. They're breaking their necks to get in, Baxter's are. There's nothing signed or sealed and you know that. Rodney Blenkinsop said he'd do this and he'd do that for me, but there's no contract. Dan Blenkinsop could back out the morrow; he could make some excuse to Mr. Rodney about it. He's in America, and it's a long way off, and I could be flat on my face before he comes back, and it would all be because my wife wouldn't allow me to speak to an attractive young lass. That's the trouble, isn't it? Because she's tall and elegant and attractive you can't bear it. Well, you might have something more to bear than that afore you've finished. You say it's up to me, and it is, and I'm telling you straight, I'm not jeopardising my future, all our futures, because you're bitchy. If she comes into the place I'm speaking to her; I say, if she comes in; it's ten-to-one she's along in the office now telling her father about the reception she got from you. And this could be the beginning of the end, Mrs. Boyle, 'cos families are funny things, especially fathers and daughters, and he thinks the sun shines out of her. Now you really have something to worry about.'

The kitchen door banged; the bottom door banged; and Mary Ann hadn't moved. For years she had prayed that some day Corny would have a break. She had seen the break as the road going through. They had bought the place eight years ago on the supposition that the by-road was going to connect the two main roads, one in and one out of the town, and thereby making the garage a thriving one. But the council had put paid to that scheme and they had merely existed for years, until the American, Mr. Blenkinsop, had come on the scene and had seen the waste land across the road as a site for his factory. And after testing Corny as to his honesty, with regard to a repair bill, he had decided to build the main gates facing the garage, and to make use of his petrol station and the spare land for garaging and lorry repairs. They had looked upon it as a sort of miracle. Now she was learning that miracles have their drawbacks, for she knew that she would give ten years of her life if the clock could be turned back for six months and Mr. Blenkinsop had decided to build his gates facing on to Riley's garage on the further road. . . .

Downstairs in the office Corny sat on the high stool, his elbows on the desk, his hand cupping his forehead. What had happened to her? This was crazy, crazy. They should be on top of the world. Instead. . . .'

'Good night, boss; I'm away.'

'Oh, good night, Jimmy. Is it that time?'

'Not me usual, but I asked you, you know. We're going to Blyth to play for a dance. I told you, you know.'

'Oh aye.' Corny nodded.

'I'll make up for it.' Jimmy hesitated in the doorway.

'Oh, that's all right, Jimmy. Go on, go on, enjoy yourself.'

'Thank you, boss. . . . Boss.' Jimmy's long body was bent forward a little.

'Yes, Jimmy?'

Jimmy lowered his head, then he rubbed his none too clean hands over his hair and said, 'Aw, it doesn't matter. Good night, boss.'

'Good night, Jimmy.'

Corny got to his feet and went into the garage, and as he did so a car came on to the drive. The driver wanted five gallons of petrol. When he went back into the office for change he pulled open the till, took out the silver and his hand moved to the side where a short while ago he had seen a ten shilling note. Now there were only pound notes. He picked up four half-crowns from the silver till and went out on to the drive.

Once more in the office he pulled the till open and looked at it. There had been a ten shilling note there just before he went upstairs. He had been checking the takings when he saw Diana crossing the drive. He had purposely gone out of the office and into the garage because he didn't want her coming in here. He didn't admit to himself the place was too small to hold both of them without coming into contact, and he feared contact with her. No petrol had been sold while he was talking to her, nor when Mary Ann came on the scene. How long had he been upstairs? Five minutes, ten minutes, not more. But Jimmy could have filled a tank during that time. Well, he could soon check on that.

He went out and looked at the registers on the tanks and when he returned the number corresponded with the amounts he had put in the book earlier.

Here was another problem.

Again he dropped his elbows on the desk and supported his head. There were only two people had access to this till, Jimmy and himself.

Jimmy had been with him since he was a nipper and he had never done this before. But there was always a first time, there was always a circumstance that pressed you just a little bit too much, and the group's car was the circumstance in Jimmy's case. But pinching from him! He had only noticed the deficiencies during the past three weeks, but it could have been going on for months, even years; not notes, but a bit of silver here and there. But now apparently he was getting reckless. Or, on the other hand—Corny's jaw tightened—he might be thinking that his boss's mind was preoccupied with other things and would be above noticing the cash desk. Aye, that was likely it. What had he wanted to say to him before he left? He'd a guilty look on his face; perhaps he had wanted to own up.

Well, there were two courses he could take. He could tackle him with it and perhaps give him the sack, or take temptation out of his way by getting a cash register in. But if he did the latter he still wouldn't be able to trust him.

Aw, God above, what with one thing and another life wasn't worth living. Why was it things had turned out like this? He had thought that when his break came he would be on top of the world; and he wasn't on top of the world, the world was on top of him.

CHAPTER FOUR

SUNDAY AFTERNOON

Sunday's pattern ran along set lines. Corny went to first Mass; the children went to ten o'clock, often accompanied by Mary Ann, after she had prepared a cold lunch to come back to.

The afternoon pattern varied slightly. Either they went to the farm or the children's grandparents visited them, or they all went to Michael's and Sarah's. Sometimes if the day was very fine the combined family would take a run out to the coast, but once a week they all met, and today Mike and Lizzie Shaughnessy were coming. Michael and Sarah would have accompanied them but they were on holiday.

At lunch Rose Mary tried to break the unhappy silence, but only succeeded in creating more tension when she remarked, 'Me granda loves Bill 'cos he's like me granda, somehow, is Bill.'

This remark had brought her mother's wrath on her and Mary Ann had exclaimed on a high note, 'Don't be ridiculous, Rose Mary. And don't dare say any such thing when your granda arrives.'

Yet when the silence fell on them again and there was only the sound of their eating and the scraping of cutlery on the plates she thought that, in a strange way, Rose Mary was right; that dog was like her father, not in looks, because it was an ugly beast, and her father, although nearing fifty, was still a handsome-looking man, but the animal had traits very like those in her da. Once he had set his mind on a thing nothing or no one would turn him away from it.

In the dog's case it was bent on making this room its headquarters. Three times this morning she had pushed him downstairs; the last time she had almost thrown him down.

At two o'clock they stood before her, all scrubbed and clean, wearing their Sunday best, and she looked from one to the other as she said, 'Now, you get messed up before your granda and grandma comes and see what I'll do.' She wagged her finger, first at Rose Mary, and then at David. 'Let him out of that shed if you dare. Mind I'm warning you.'

As they stared back at her she read their minds. 'She's cruel. Mam's cruel.'

The phone ringing broke their concentration; the phone was connected with the office downstairs and Corny was downstairs. Mary Ann hesitated a moment before picking it up, and then his voice came to her.

'Your mother's just phoned. She say's Gran's arrived; she'll have to bring her along.'

Mary Ann closed her eyes.

'Are you there?'

She forced herself to say 'Yes.' Where did he think she was?

'Look, honey.' His voice was low. 'This has got to stop.'

She glanced round at the children. They were both still looking at her, and she motioned them away with her hand, and as they went out of the door she said stiffly into the phone, 'I didn't start it.'

'Well, neither did I. Look, love, I tell you there's not a thing in it. Believe me. . . . Look, your mam and dad's coming; they'll smell a rat if we go on like this.'

'Is that all you're afraid of?'

The shout he gave into the phone made her pull her head sharply back.

'I'm afraid of nothing. I've told you I've done nothing to be afraid of. You'd drive a man mad. I'm tellin' you mind, if you go on like this you'll get what you're askin' for.'

When she heard the phone being banged down she put the receiver back and put her hand up to her lips to stop their trembling. She had her head bowed as she went on to the landing but she brought it up with a jerk when she saw the two of them standing looking at her. The next minute they were on her. Their arms about her, their heads buried in her waist, they enfolded her in silent sympathy, and she had to bite tight on her lips to stop herself from breaking down.

'Come on. Come on.' She ruffled their heads; then exclaimed, 'Aw, now look what I've gone and done, and me going for you to keep tidy.' She looked down into their faces, and they stared back at her. Then she said brokenly, 'Come on, I'll tidy you up,' and, still clinging to her, they went into the bedroom. And as she combed their hair she thought, They're so big a part of me, there's nothing I think that they don't sense and she pulled them towards her again and kissed them one after the other. And then she was crying softly, and Rose Mary was crying softly, and David was blinking hard and sucking his bottom lip right into his mouth.

'If you wanted a dog, why didn't you get a dog, not an ugly beast like that?' Gran was addressing Mary Ann pointedly, and Mary Ann, as always, was praying that she be given the power to answer her grandmother civilly. This woman who had been the torment of her da's life, the thorn in the side of her mother, and the constant pinprick—and that was putting it mildly—in her own.

Grandma McMullen never seemed to get any older. Her well-preserved body, her jet black hair piled high on her head, her thick-skinned face and round black eyes looked ageless. Mary Ann could never imagine her dying, although she wished it every time they met; but this, she knew, was the vainest of all her wishes.

She replied to her now, 'I didn't want the dog; I didn't bring it here.'

'Oh! Oh!' Mrs. McMullen swung her head widely, taking in her daughter, Lizzie and her son-in-law Mike, and Corny, and then she appealed to an invisible figure standing somewhere near the window. 'Did you hear that? The world is coming to an end; somebody's got one over on her at last. . . .'

As Mary Ann went into the scullery, Lizzie rose to her feet, saying, 'You're in one of your good moods today, aren't you, Mother?' Then she went hastily towards the door between the kitchen and scullery and closed it and, coming towards her mother again, ended, 'Now I warned you before we came away, no one's got to put up with your tongue.'

Mrs. McMullen slowly bowed her head, then brought it up sideways and again she appealed to the imaginary figure near the window, 'Well! Do you hear that?' she said. 'Do you hear that? It's come to something when you can't open your mouth. Look.' She now confronted her daughter with a hard black stare. 'I was meaning to be funny. Hasn't anybody got a sense of humour around here?'

'You could have fooled me.'

'What!' The old lady turned and glared at her son-in-law's back as it moved towards the door leading out on to the landing, and as Mike went through it she said in no small voice, 'Yes, I could have fooled you; it wouldn't take much to do that.'

Lizzie almost sprang towards the other door now and, banging it closed, she cried under her breath, 'Now that's finished it. Now I warned you; this is the last time you come out with us.'

Mrs. McMullen stared at her daughter again. Then, her head wagging and her mouth working as if she was chewing on gum, she said, 'You were glad enough to come in me car.'

'Oh, my goodness!' Lizzie put her hand to her head and was about to turn from her mother but confronted her again, crying, 'Your reasoning has always been a mystery to me, Mother. It still is. We've got a car of our own; we didn't need yours to come in. You got Fred Tyler to bring you to the farm today so that Corny could look it over.'

'No such thing. Who told you that?'

'Fred Tyler told me that, if you want to know. You told him it would be a free ride as he wanted to visit his folks in Felling.'

'He's a liar.'

'Oh well, that's all right then, he's a liar and you don't want Corny to look her over.' She glanced swiftly at Corny, and Corny who had remained silent all this while looked at Gran, and Gran looked at him, and after a moment she said, 'I'll pay you; I don't want you to do it for nothing. But those other beggars in Shields, they sting me to death. They sent me in a

53

bill for seven pounds. Where am I going to find seven pounds?'

Before Corny could answer, Lizzie said, 'You shouldn't be keeping the car, you can't afford to run it. You know you can't. You should have sold it the minute you won it. Now it's going to rack and ruin standing outside your front door. What do you want with a car, anyway, at your age?'

'It's my car and I'll keep it as long as I like, and I'll thank you to mind your own business. As for age; if you had half as much life in you as I have you'd be more spry than you are now.'

As Lizzie looked down on her mother she wondered how, during all these long years of torment, she had prevented herself from striking her; for most of her life she'd had this kind of thing to deal with. Age had not softened her mother or changed her, except for the worst.

'What's wrong with her?' asked Corny flatly now.

'I don't know. That's what you'll have to find out. She goes pink-pink-pink-pink, like that. Fred Tayler says he thinks it's just due to verberration.'

'Verberration? You mean vibration.'

'I mean verberration. That's what he said. I'm not daft.'

No, she wasn't daft, not her. Corny, looking down on Mrs. McMullen, hardened his heart enough to say, 'If it's anything big I won't be able to tackle her; I've got too much in.'

'How can it be anything big, it was new only a few months ago.'

'Lots of things go wrong with new cars.'

'Not with this one. You said it was one of the best.'

'So it is. But still things can go wrong. And I'm telling you, if it's anything that's going to take time you'll have to get it fixed elsewhere.'

He felt mean acting like this, but once he started doing her repairs she'd never be off the door. When she had won the car he had offered to buy it from her, but no; and now it was being ruined standing out in all weathers and had depreciated by hundreds already. He turned abruptly and went out.

On the drive he found Mike. He was standing quietly smoking and looking towards the chaotic jumble of machinery on

54

the other side of the road; he grinned at him and said, 'I suppose you know by now why she came. She's after you for free repairs. If you once start she'll have you at it.'

'She'll not. I told her, if it's anything big she can take it elsewhere.'

'Aw, she's a crafty old bitch if ever there was one.' Mike squared his teeth on the stem of his pipe, then turned and walked with Corny towards the Wolseley. But before Corny lifted the bonnet he said, 'I'd better put on a set of overalls else I'll get me head in me hands.'

When he returned and began to tap various parts of the car engine, Mike stood watching him in silence for a few minutes, then he asked casually, 'What's up, Corny?'

Corny's eyes flicked towards Mike; then he turned his attention again to the car. You couldn't keep much from Mike; in any case, the feeling between himself and Mary Ann was sticking out like a sore thumb.

'Serious?' asked Mike quietly.

'Could be.' There was a pause before Corny straightened himself and, looking at Mike, said, 'She's mad.'

Mike was smiling tolerantly. 'Haven't noticed it up to now. Quick-tempered like. Takes after her male parent'—his smile widened—'but mad? Well——' he shook his head—'what's made her mad, Corny?'

'Come in here a minute.' Corny led the way into his office, where, having closed the door, he confronted Mike and said plainly. 'She thinks I'm gone on somebody else.'

They stared at each other. They were both about the same height, touching six foot two, and they could have been father and son in that their hair was almost the same hue of red. But whereas Corny's body was thin and sinewy, Mike's was heavily built.

Mike took the pipe from his mouth and tapped it against the palm of his hand, but still kept his eyes on Corny as he asked quietly, 'Well, are you?'

Corny tossed his head. It was an impatient gesture, and it was some seconds before he said 'Look; it's like this, Mike.' He now went on to explain how Diana Blenkinsop came into the picture, and when he had finished there was a long pause before Mike said, 'Well, as I see it, she's got a point, Corny. Oh! Oh!' he held up his hand. 'Hold your horses; don't go down me throat. I've been through this meself, you remember?' His mouth moved up at one corner. 'It nearly spoilt your wedding. I don't need to go through all that again, do I? But I'm just telling you I know how you feel. . . .'

'But Mike, man, I don't really feel anything for her, not really. She's nice to natter to, she gives you a sort of kick. . . . Well. . . .' Again he tossed his head. 'When anybody seeks you out it gives you a kick whether it's man, woman or child. You know that yourself.'

'Aye, as you say, I know that meself; but I'm going to say this to you, Corny. It's a dangerous game to play. But for Mary Ann confronting me with the truth about that little bitch who had almost hypnotised me, well I don't know where I'd be the day. It was a sort of madness. At least it was in my case; I was clawing my way back to youth, willing my dreams to take shape in the daylight. Aw, lad, I know all about it. But in your case you haven't reached that stage yet; you're young. But young or not, this could be serious. You know, Mary Ann's nature is like a fiddle string, the slightest touch and it vibrates. God forgive me, but I made it vibrate more than enough when she was young. I was a heart scald to her, and she doesn't want to go through that again, Corny, not in any way.'

Corny sat slowly down on the high stool and he bowed his head as he said, 'You know how I feel about her. I don't need to put it into words; you know the whole story. Every since I was an ignorant nipper, a loud-mouth lout, she has stood by me, defended me, and I could have loved her for that alone, but I loved her for herself. I still do. God, she knows it. But Mike, that doesn't mean to say I daren't look at another lass.'

'No, no, it doesn't; of course it doesn't. . . . What does she look like, this Diana Blenkinsop?'

Corny raised his eyebrows and smiled wryly. 'The lot. Straight off the front of a magazine. Long legs, no bust, flaxen hair down her back, blue eyes, red lips, and five foot ten.'

Mike took the flat of his hand and flapped it against his brow as he said, 'And you wonder why she's up in the air. Why man, you know she hates being small, and for you to look at anybody an inch taller would be enough, but five foot ten, and all that thrown in, aw, Corny, that isn't playing the game.'

'Well,' Corny got up from the seat and his voice was serious, 'game or no game, Mike, I've got to be civil to her; she's Dan Blenkinsop's daughter and he's in charge here while Mr. Rodney's in America. Even when he's back Dan'll still be in charge. As I tried to explain to Mary Ann, at this stage he could make me or break me.'

'And so you've got to suck up to his daughter.'

'NO!' The word was a bark. 'And don't use that expression to me, Mike. I suck up to nobody; never have. If I'd been that way inclined I'd be further on the day, I suppose.'

'I'm sorry, Corny.' Mike put his hand on Corny's shoulder. 'I shouldn't have put it like that, it was too raw. But you feel you've got to be nice to her?'

Corny's face was sullen and his lips were tight as he said, 'I feel I haven't got to do as me wife says and tell her to stay to hell out of the garage, and when she brings a message from her father I haven't got to say to her, "Look I don't want anything by hand, use the phone." '

'Aye. Aye, I know it's awkward, but remember, Corny, Mary Ann's got her side to it. Anyway, we all run into patches like this, and they pass.'

'Patches! They're more than patches that hit me. My life is either as dull as ditch water with nothing happening, or everything's coming at me from all sides at once. I've got another thing on my mind and all ... Jimmy.'

'Jimmy?'

'Aye, he's helping himself to bits of cash.' He nodded towards the till.

'Jimmy! I can't believe that; he's a good lad. I would have said he's as straight as a die.'

'So would I, staked me life on it; but he's after a car. That gang of his want a new van to hold them and their instruments, and naturally he's expected to pig in. If he was on his own he likely could, but with his mother to see to money's tight. I've given him two ten bob rises this year, I can't give him any more at the present. I've promised him I'll put him on a better basis at the end of the year. I'll know where I stand then. The factory should be up and if I get my way I'll be under contract to Blenkinsop, Mr. Rodney, not Dan, and then to hell with them all. But in the meantime I'm not putting Jimmy's money up and then not being able to pull it down again if things don't go the way they should.'

'Aye, I see your point, but I wouldn't have believed it about Jimmy if you hadn't told me yourself. You've got proof?'

'Well, there's ten shilling notes been slipping away once or twice a week. I haven't kept tag on the silver, the Lord knows how much of that's gone.... Aw come on.' He moved towards the door. 'I'd better see to the old faggot's machine.'

As they went on to the drive again the children came tearing round the end of the garage, with Bill on their heels, and Rose Mary cried, 'Granda! Granda! Look at him jumping. Up Bill! Up Bill!' She held her hand brow high and Bill leapt at it, but when he dropped to the ground again he fell on his side and rolled on to his back, and Mike laughed and Corny was forced to smile. 'It's his legs,' he said ... 'they just won't hold that chest of his. That's why we got him. He was the runt. But runt or not, he's a thoroughbred, he's a good dog, Mike.'

Mike, looking at Bill, nodded, saying, 'Yes, he looks a fine fellow. I wouldn't like him to get a hold of my leg when he's a few months older. Just look at those jaws.'

As the children dashed away again with Bill tearing after them, Corny said, 'She hates the sight of him.'

'Well, you can't say he's a pretty dog; women like something nice to look at.'

'Nice to look at!' Corny jerked his chin. 'That dog's got character.' He now turned and grinned widely at Mike and there was a chuckle in his voice as he said, 'I'll say he has. Oh lad, if you could have seen the kitchen on that first night you would have thought a ship load of rats had been at it.' He gave a deep gurgle. 'She nearly went daft. Mind, I could have killed him meself, but after, when I thought about it, I had to laugh. He reminded me of Joe. Do you remember the dog I had as a lad? I used to bring him to me grannie's.'

'Oh, Joe. Oh yes, I remember you and Joe. Didn't you nearly break Fanny's neck with him once?'

'Yes, I had him on a piece of rope and there was a kid from

upstairs came in. She had a cat in her arms and Joe dived and hurled me across the room, and he took me grannie's legs from under her, and she grabbed at the tablecloth as she went down. She had just put out four plates of stew. Oh, I never forget that night.' He was laughing loudly. 'I can see her, to this day, sitting on the floor covered in it, and Joe, flat out under the table, looking at her. Eeh! my, we had to run. And I daren't show me face in the door for days after. . . . But it might have killed her, the fall she took.'

They were both laughing now.

'It would take more than that to kill Fanny,' said Mike. 'By the way, how is she?'

'Oh, grand. I saw her last week. She's got a new lease of life. Going to bingo now.'

'No!'

'Aye; she had won thirty-six bob and she was standing treats as it was thirty-six thousand. You know her.'

'Oh aye, I know Fanny. I wish there were more like her. . . .'

It was about half-an-hour later when Lizzie put her head out of the window and called, 'Tea's ready!' and Mike called back, 'Coming!' Then looking at Corny, who was still tinkering with the engine, he said, 'I would leave that and let her get on with it, we'd better not keep them waiting, we don't want any more black looks.' Then turning 'round, he called, 'Rose Mary! David! Come on; tea up.'

'Granda! Dad!' Rose Mary came running up to the car. 'Have you seen Bill?'

Corny brought his head up so quickly from the engine that it bumped the top of the bonnet, and, rubbing it, he screwed up his face as he said. 'Have we seen Bill? You're asking me when you've had him all afternoon?'

'Well, he was with us a minute ago and now he's gone.' She looked over the road and called, 'Is he there, David?' and David came running and shouting, 'No, I can't see him.'

'Where had you him last?' asked Mike, and Rose Mary answered, 'Down in the field, Granda. We came round the back way and on to the drive, and we thought he'd be here.'

'Oh Lord!' Corny covered his face with one hand, then,

oblivious of the grease on it, he pushed it upwards through his hair and said, 'Take ten to one he's upstairs.'

'No.' Mike moved quickly now towards the door of the house, saying, 'I'm going to enjoy this.'

'You'll be the only one then,' said Corny, pulling off his overalls and throwing them into the front of the garage.

When he reached the stairs he expected to find Mary Ann at the top with the dog by the scruff of the neck, but there was no one to be seen, not even Mike or the children.

On entering the kitchen he stood within the door taking in the scene. Bill was seated inside the fender, his rump to the stove that housed a back boiler and was comfortably warm. His mouth was wide open, his tongue lolling out of one side, and with his small round black eyes he was appraising the company, one after the other.

Lizzie stood staring down at him. Mary Ann, too, stood staring at him, but from the distance of the scullery doorway, her mouth grim, one hand on her hip, her pose alone spelling battle. The children stood close to Mike by the side of the table, their attention riveted on Bill.

And Mrs. McMullen. Well, Mrs. McMullen sat in the big chair to the side of the fireplace and she glared at Bill, and her look seemed to bring his eyes to focus finally on her, and as they stared at each other she passed sentence. 'Dogs like him want puttin' down when they're young,' she said: 'they're a dangerous breed, they can't be trusted with children. Once they get their teeth in they hang on. Killed a bairn they did. It was in the papers not so long ago. Just give him another couple of months, and you won't be able to do anything with him, you'll find yourself in Court with a summons and a hospital bill to pay for somebody's leg, that is if he hasn't finished them off.'

'He could be trained,' said Lizzie.

'What, to finish them off?' laughed Mike.

Lizzie ignored this and, looking at her mother, said, 'Give him a chance, he's only a puppy.'

'Puppy! He's as big as a house end now, what'll he be like when he's fully grown? This poky room won't hold him. It doesn't hold much now, but wait till he's reached his size. . . .'

'Then we'll move into a bigger house to accommodate him.'

They now all looked at Corny as he moved past Mary Ann and went into the scullery to wash his hands.

'Oh, you're all going to break eggs with a big stick. You're a long time moving into your bigger houses.'

As the kettle boiled Mary Ann went to the gas stove and from there she heard Corny mutter over the sink, 'Break eggs with a big stick, the old buzzard!'

If only everything had been all right, Mary Ann knew that at this minute she would have been standing close to his side and he would have made her giggle. She also knew that she would even have taken Bill's part, simply because her grannie didn't like him.

As she made the tea Corny stood drying his hands watching her, and when she went to pass him to get the tea stand from the cupboard he suddenly caught her by the arm, and they stared at each other for a moment; then quickly his mouth dropped on hers, hard, possessively. When he looked at her again her eyes were gushing tears and he put his arms about her, whispering. 'Don't. Don't. Don't let her see you crying, for God's sake; that'll give her too much satisfaction. Go on. Go on.' He pushed her towards the sink. 'See to your face, I'll take the tea in.'

As he passed her with the tray he put out his free hand and touched her hair, and this did not help to ease her crying.

'You didn't tell me what was wrong with her, the car?' Gran greeted him as he entered the room again, and he said, 'It was a hole in the exhaust; I've done what I can.'

'How much will it be?'

'I'll send me bill in,' he said.

'Well, don't forget,' she answered.

It would just serve her damn well right if he did send a bill in. And wouldn't she get a shock? He could imagine her coming storming up here, raising the roof on him.

The talk was falsely animated during the meal. It was Corny who kept the conversation going, and in this he was aided by Mike.

Mary Ann, from her place at the bottom of the table, poured out the tea, and from her seat, if she cast her eyes to

61

the right, she could see Bill. He had settled down by the stove with his head lying on his front paws. He looked utterly relaxed. She found herself wishing she could like him; she wished she could put up with him for everybody's sake, especially now that her grannie couldn't stand him. There must be something good about the beast if her grannie didn't like him.

There was always a climax when Mrs. McMullen visited her relations. It came earlier than usual during this visit, just as tea was finished.

It should happen that Bill had found the stove slightly too warm for his thin coat and had moved from the inside of the fender to the outside, and this brought him to the foot of 'Gran's chair'. When she left the table and went to sit down there was Bill. He was not impeding her; she could have sat down and not even touched him, but that wasn't Gran's way. Taking her foot, she gave him a sharp dig in the ribs. The result was surprising but, as she herself had stated earlier, predictable.

Bill had been happy today, as he had never been since he had left his mother. He was in a warm place which was permeated with nice smells. He had discovered he was very fond of biscuits, not the broken biscuits that you got with your dinner, but biscuits with chocolate on them. He knew he was going to develop a real taste for biscuits with chocolate on them. Chocolate had a particular smell and there was a strong smell of chocolate in this room. He knew that if he waited long enough and quietly enough he would be rewarded. That was, until the thing hit him in the ribs. His reaction to the pain was for his jaws to spring open, then snap closed, and to give vent to a cry that was part yelp, part yap and part growl, and all the time he felt the pain he jumped madly around the room dodging under one object after another.

'There! There! What did I tell you? He's dangerous. He went for me.'

'He did no such thing!' Lizzie was yelling at her mother. 'You asked for it.'

'I asked for what?'

'You should have left him alone.'

'Don't chase him, let up,' cried Corny.

'Look, stop it!' Mary Ann was shouting at the twins now. 'You'll have the things off the table.'

'Here he is! Here he is!' Mike reached down behind the couch and grabbed at Bill's collar, and, pulling him up, he thrust him wriggling and squirming into David's arms and David, now looking fearfully up at his mother, said, 'He didn't do it. He didn't start it, Mam, it was Gran. She kicked him. I saw her; she kicked him.'

'I did nothing of the sort, boy. Well! would you believe it?'

'Yes, you did, Gran, I saw you.' Rose Mary was now standing by David's side confronting the old woman, and Mrs. McMullen, looking from one to the other of her great-grandchildren, didn't know which she disliked most, or whether her dislike for them was greater than that for their mother. But that couldn't possibly be. Nevertheless, she knew that there was a time when it was advisable to retreat, and so with great dignity she sat down in her chair again and, her chin moving upwards, she made a statement, which was sinisterly prophetic in this case.

'Every dog has his day,' she said.

David stared at her; then grinning he said flippantly, 'Aye, and a bitch has two afternoons.'

Such a reply coming from her great-grandson not only brought Mrs. McMullen's eyebrows almost up to her hairline but also created an amazed silence in the room, and an assortment of astounded expressions.

Still holding on to the wriggling dog, David now looked apprehensively from one face to the other. He'd get wrong, he knew he would. He felt a little afraid, until all of a sudden there came a sound like an explosion. It was his granda and his dad bursting out laughing together. His granda had his hand on his dad's shoulder and he was roaring. And his grandma too, she was laughing with her head down and her face covered. But his mam wasn't laughing. The next minute she had hold of his collar and was pushing him and Bill outside while Rose Mary came after them shouting, 'No Mam. No Mam.'

On the landing, Mary Ann looked down at her son and

hissed under her breath, 'David! where on earth did you hear that?'

'It . . . it wasn't swearin', Mam.'

Mary Ann swallowed deeply. 'It was a kind of swearing.'

At this David shook his head and glanced at Rose Mary, and Rose Mary said, 'Not really, Mam, not proper swearin'.'

'Who told you it?'

David blinked and hitched Bill further up into his arms and had to avoid his licking tongue before he said, 'Nobody, Mam; I just heard it.'

'Where?'

David glanced at Rose Mary again, then looked down but didn't answer, and Mary wanted to take him by the shoulders and shake him. But that meant shaking that animal too and then anything might happen. 'Where?' she repeated.

It was Rose Mary who answered for him. 'Jimmy. Jimmy says that, Mam.'

Mary Ann straightened herself up. Jimmy? Well, wait until she saw him tomorrow. 'Take that animal downstairs and lock him up,' she said.

Neither of them moved. They were looking up at her, blinking all the while.

'You heard what I said.'

'She kicked him, Mam. He wouldn't have done anything if she hadn't have kicked him.' As David spoke the door opened and Corny and Mike came on to the landing. They were still laughing. Mary Ann did not look at them but at the children and repeated, 'Take him downstairs.'

They both glanced at their father and grandfather, then went slowly down the stairs, and Mary Ann turned and looked at these two whom she loved so deeply that the feeling often brought nothing but pain, and she saw them now as a couple of boys. They were leaning against each other and she hissed at them under her breath, 'Stop it! D'you hear? Stop it!'

Mike now put his hand out towards her, spluttering, 'And a bitch has two afternoons.'

As she saw their laughter mounting she pushed them towards the bedroom, and once inside she cried, 'If you must act like bairns do it in here.'

64

'She ... she wants her hat and coat,' Mike gasped; 'she's going ... we're going. We're going out on a wave. We always go out on a wave when she's about.'

She picked up her grannie's coat and went out and into the kitchen, there to be met by the standing figure of Mrs. McMullen.

Mary Ann didn't hand her grannie her hat and coat; instead, she handed them to her mother, and it was Lizzie who went to help the old lady into her things, only to be repulsed with the words, 'Thank you! I can see to meself.'

And that was all Mrs. McMullen said until they reached the bottom of the stairs, and there, turning and looking straight into Mary Ann's face, she remarked, 'They're a credit to you. They're a pair you could take anywhere. You must be proud of them.'

The pressure of her mother's fingers on her arm stilled her retort, and Lizzie, bending down, kissed her and whispered, 'I'll ring you later.'

When her da kissed her his eyes were still wet and gleaming, but he said nothing more, he just patted her cheek and went towards the car.

She did not wait to see them off but returned upstairs, and a few minutes later Corny entered the room. He came straight towards her, the twinkle deep in his eye, but he did not repeat the joke; instead, he picked her up in his arms as he had been wont to do and sat down with her in the big chair, and when he pressed her face into his neck her body began to shake, but not with laughter; she was picking up where she had left off in the scullery earlier on.

CHAPTER FIVE

GETTING ACQUAINTED

'Now Rose Mary, if I've told you once I've told you a hundred times, he can't come upstairs; he's all right where he is.'

'But listen to him, Mam, he's yelling the place down. He's lonely. He likes people, he does; he only cries when he's by hisself. . . .'

Mary Ann had turned her head away, but now she brought her gaze down to her daughter again as she said patiently, 'He's a puppy, Rose Mary, he's got to learn. He won't learn if you give in to him.'

Rose Mary's lips trembled as she muttered, 'I worry all day 'bout him, shut up in there in the dark. I'm frightened of the dark, you know I am, Mam, and he——'

'Rose Mary!' It came on a high note, but when she saw her daugher's face crumpling into tears she knew that this would continue all the way to school, and all during Miss Plum's questioning, and she was forced to compromise. 'Look,' she said; 'you can go and let him out. He can run round behind the garage, but see that the lane gate is closed, for mind'—she bent down towards her daughter—'if he gets out on the road among all those lorries he could be killed.'

'Yes, I know, Mam. All right, Mam, I'll fasten the gate tight.' Swiftly now Rose Mary's arms came up and hugged her mother around the neck. 'Thanks, Mam. . . Ta. I'll tell our David.'

David was standing in grim silence at the bottom of the stairs waiting for her, and she dashed at him, whispering hoarsely, 'Mam says we can let him out and he can run in the back.'

'She did?'

'Yes. Come on, hurry, 'cos we'll miss the bus else.'

They raced round the side of the building, through the wooden gate that was laced with wire netting, and to the woodshed, and when they released Bill he showed his thanks by bounding around them until David grabbed his collar and, pressing on his hindquarters to keep him still, said, 'Now look; you behave yourself and we'll take you out the night, eh?' He wanted to rub his face against the dog but refrained. But Rose Mary, dropping on to her hunkers, cupped the long snout in her hands, and as she bent to kiss it the slobbering tongue covered her face in one stroke from chin to brow, and she almost fell over laughing.

When they ran to the gate Bill galloped with them, but when he realised he wasn't going to be allowed through he stood up on his hind legs against the wire netting and howled. He howled and he howled until gradually he tired and then he reduced his howling to a whimper before turning forlornly away to investigate the open area.

He found it a place of little interest, except for the wooden wals of the garage out of which a number of quaint smells oozed, none of them very alluring. The investigation over, he returned to the gate and discovered that if he kept to one side of it he could see occasional activity on a small patch of road fronting the garage. It was as he lay gazing in this direction, and bored to extinction, that he saw coming towards him an apparition which brought his body springing upwards. When the apparition reached the other side of the gate and pressed its nose against the wire netting and so touched his, the effect was like an electric shock. It shot up his bony muzzle, along his spine and right to the end of his tail, where it recharged itself and retraced its path.

Bill hadn't seen one of his own kind since he had left his family, and now he was being confronted by a female. That she wasn't of his own breed, nor yet could lay claim to being a thoroughbred didn't trouble him. He couldn't have cared less that she wasn't a simple cross between a poodle and a terrier, and that obvious other breeds could be detected in her ancestry; to him she was the most fascinating creature he had

67

encountered so far in his young life, and urges, entirely new to him, were acting like crossed wires under his coat, for ripples of delight were darting off at tangents through every part of his body.

He said a breathless, 'Hello,' and she answered with a cool, 'Hello'. And then she indicated by turning her back on him and taking a few steps from the gate that she wouldn't mind if he accompanied her.

There was nothing Bill wanted more at this moment than to accompany this witch, and when she returned to the gate, squatted, and gave him absolute proof of her feeling for him, there arose in him a blind fury against the barrier between them, and nothing or no one was going to prevent him from breaking it down. To this end he got his teeth into the bottom strand of the wire netting and he pulled, and he tugged and he bit while the temptress walked up and down on the other side of the gate giving him encouragement in the way she knew best.

When Bill had made a hole big enough to get his head through the lady walked away again, and when she realised he wasn't following she stood looking at him in some disappointment; then, like many another lady before her, she suddenly got fed up with the whole business and trotted off.

Bill, now working with intensified fury, enlarged the hole, and with a wriggle he was through. Like lightning he was on the garage drive, then on the road, and across it. He pulled up once to sniff at what was left of a thorn bush, which confirmed that she had passed this way, and then he was running amidst the tangle of building material, cranes, grabs and lorries. . . .

Mary Ann was feeling somewhat better this morning, though not exactly light in heart; she would never feel like that again until Miss Blenkinsop decided to take a position elsewhere, and as things stood she couldn't see her doing that. But last night Corny had been his old self and he had assured her that in the whole wide world she was the only one that mattered to him, and she believed him. But that was last night, in the darkness, with her head buried on his chest; this morning, in the stark light of day, and the time approaching ten minutes to nine when Miss Blenkinsop would be arriving, bringing her car on the drive with a flourish and pulling up, with a screech of brakes, at the garage door, she wasn't so sure. Anyway madam would be disappointed this morning, for it would be Jimmy who would take her car and park it in the garage, because Corny had gone into Shields on business.

Even knowing that she wouldn't witness Corny greeting Diana Blenkinsop as he did most mornings, Mary Ann found herself standing to the side of the front room window which overlooked the drive. She wondered what madam would be wearing this morning; perhaps a mini skirt. No, she wouldn't dare wear a mini skirt, not with her height.

The drive was empty of cars and people, and after a moment Mary Ann's gaze was drawn across the road and to a section practically opposite the window, where last week they had started to excavate the land prior to building an underground car park beneath one of the factory shops. The excavations had reached the point where the hole was about twenty feet deep. On the edge of it a grab was working. At present it was stationary. Her eyes were passing over it when they were brought leaping back to take in a black and white figure standing on top of the grab itself.

Bill! No, it couldn't be, he was in the yard. But ... but there was only one Bill, there could only be one Bill hereabouts and that was him. He had got out. Then something happened that caused her to push up the window and yell at the top of her voice, 'Stop it! Stop it!'

As she ran down the stairs she could still see the wide grin on the grab operator's face as he leant from the cab pointing out the dog to his mates, and even before he pulled the lever gently to set the grab in motion Mary Ann had known what he was about to do.

When she reached the driveway she saw the grab swinging into mid-air, with the petrified dog clinging with its two front paws to one of the supporting chains, while its hind legs slithered here and there on the muddy surface of the lid. The operator was doing it for a laugh. If he opened the grab the dog would fall between the lips, but he was just having a laugh and the men on the rim were guffawing loudly.

'Stop it! Stop it this minute!' She was below the cab now

yelling up at the man. 'You cruel, sadistic devil, you! Stop it, I tell you.'

'What do you say, missus?'

The grin was wider now.

'You heard what I said. You'll hear of this. That's my dog.'

'He's all right; he's just havin' an obstacle put in his way, he's after a bitch. He's all right.' The man flapped his hand at her.

'You'll be far from all right when my husband finishes with you.'

'Oh aye? Just make the appointment then, missus, just make the appointment. Tell him any time.'

'Stop that thing.'

'I'd better not, missus. Better get it to the bottom, break his neck else. Would you like his neck broke?'

When the grab hit the bottom of the hole she watched Bill fall off into the mud, then make an attempt to crawl out of it. But the harder he paddled the more he stuck.

'Oh, you're a horrible swine. That's what you are, a horrible swine.' There were tears in her voice as she yelled, not only at the crane man now but at the men standing further along the rim. Then before anyone knew what she was up to she was slipping and sliding down the wet clay face of the hole.

May Ann wasn't aware of the scene behind her now, but a man in a trilby hat and leather jacket had come up to the crane demanding, 'What's this? What's up?'

'Aw, it was just a joke.'

'A joke?' The man bawled. 'What's that woman doing down there? What's this anyway?'

'The dog was on the grab,' one of the men put in sheepishly, 'and Sam let him down.'

'You did what!' The man looked up at the operator.

'He's not hurt. He was just sitting there and I set it moving.'

The two men stared at one another for a moment; then the man in the trilby hat said, 'I'll bloody well set you moving after this.' Then going over the rim himself, he reached Mary Ann just as she fell flat on her face in the quagmire with Bill in her arms.

When he pulled her to her feet he said, 'Give him here.' But Bill refused to be parted from Mary Ann. His whole body quivering, he clung on to the shoulder of her dress and as the man's hands came on him he made a pitiful sound and Mary Ann gasped, 'It's all right, I can manage him.'

'Look; you'll have to let me help you; you can't walk in this.' Without further words he put his arm around her waist and lifted her sucking feet from out of the mud, and like a mother carrying a child on her hip he bore her to the far side of the hole where the ground was comparatively dry, then mounted a ladder that had been laid against the sloping ground.

When he reached the rim he put her on her feet and steadied her, saying, 'There, there; you're all right.'

'Th-thank you.'

''Struth! we're in a mess.' He knocked lumps of mud from his jacket, then added, 'Somebody'll pay for this. Come on.'

As they walked back around the perimeter of the hole he said, 'You're Mrs. Boyle, aren't you? Used to be Shaughnessy?'

'Yes. Yes, that's right.'

'You don't remember me? Aw well, it's not the time to press an introduction. You'd better get yourself into the house and get that stuff off you, and him.' He nodded towards Bill who was still clinging tenaciously to Mary Ann's shoulder.

Mary Ann looked at her rescuer. She didn't remember ever having seen him before; but then his face was all bespattered and his clothes were in a similar plight to her own, which made her say, 'I think you need cleaning up an' all. Would you like to come inside? You're about the same build as ... as my husband, you could have a change of clothes if you like.'

'Well, that's very nice of you. I wouldn't mind getting out of this clobber at the moment.'

When they came to the grab the operator was busily at work, as were his mates, and the man muttered, 'I'll see to them later.'

There were two other people who had witnessed the incident, Jimmy and Diana Blenkinsop. Jimmy, his long face stretched even to a greater length, said, 'Eeh! Mrs. Boyle, you

71

shouldn't have gone down there.'

Diana Blenkinsop gave a little laugh, and she said, 'You have got yourself into a mess, haven't you? He would have got out on his own you know; he comes of a very tenacious breed.'

'AND SO DO I!' said Mary Ann, pausing slightly before marching across the road, followed by the man.

When they reached the drive he said under his breath, 'Friend of yours?'

'What do you think?' She glanced sideways at him, and he grinned back at her, and the grin stirred a faint memory in her mind. She had seen him before but she couldn't place him.

After scraping their feet on the scraper let into the wall, she led the way upstairs, and on the landing she pointed to a door, saying, 'That's the bathroom. There's plenty of hot water. I'll bring you some clean clothes as soon as I get the thick off.'

'Don't hurry.' He was grinning again. 'And I think you'd better start on the bold boy first; if you let him down he'll leave you some trade marks.'

'Yes, you're right.' She laughed at the man. She liked his voice, his easy manner. He was nice.

In the scullery, when she attempted to put Bill into the sink he dug his claws into her shoulder again and hung on to her, and she stroked his muddy head with her equally muddy hand and said, 'It's all right. It's all right, I won't hurt you.'

When finally she had him standing in the sink he sat down quite suddenly as if his legs would no longer support him, and when he looked up at her and made a little whining sound she laughed again and said, 'It's all right, I'm not going to drown you.'

When he was clean she put him inside the fender and, pressing him firmly downwards, commanded sternly, 'Now stay. Stay. I'll be back.' Then she scrambled into the bedroom, whipped some clean things for herself out of the wardrobe, together with a shirt and old trousers and a coat of Corny's, and going to the bathroom door called, 'I'm leaving the things outside.'

The voice came to her cheerily, 'Right-o. Thanks. Thanks a lot. I could stay in here all day.'

As she heard the swish of water she smiled and hurried into

the scullery again, and there she stripped her clothes off, washed her face, legs and arms in the sink, and got into her clean clothes; and she was in the kitchen again before a tap came on the door.

When he entered the room she looked at him and laughed with him as he said, 'All made to measure. Would you believe it? Except that your man's a bit longer in the leg than me, we must be of a size.'

'You are.' She nodded at him. 'Would you like a drink of something, I've got the kettle on?'

'Now that's very nice of you, but I should be getting back, that lot will be having a holiday knowing I'm out of the way for five minutes.... On the other hand, they'll be expecting me to blow me top and are likely playing wary, so yes, thanks, I'll take that drink.'

He sat down by the side of the table and as she went into the scullery he called to her, 'His nibs has settled down all right, not a peep out of him.'

'I think he's still suffering from shock,' she called back.

'Well, aye, it would be a shock to the poor little beggar to find himself whisked into mid-air like that. That Fred Tyler's an empty-headed nowt, if ever there was one. If it had been his mother on top of the grab he would have done the same. By the way, don't you remember me?'

She came to the scullery door and stared at him. Yes, yes, she had seen him somewhere before. He was a very attractive looking fellow; black hair, deep brown eyes, squarish face, well built.

'Fillimore Street. You know, behind Burton Street and Mulhattan's Hall. We used to live next to the Scallans, the daughter who married Jack McBride. They were Salvationists, and old Fanny nearly went barmy.'

'Murgatroyd!' Mary Ann was pointing at him, her finger wagging. 'Yes, yes, of course, Murgatroyd. Johnny Murgatroyd, of course.'

'I used to chase you round the back lanes and try to scare the wits out of you.'

She laughed widely as she recalled the big lanky fellow swooping down on her from the street corner when she was returning from school; especially would he swoop on St. Patrick's Day, because she was green and he was blue.

She brought the cups of coffee to the table, and as she sat down she said, 'Well, well, after all these years, and you've got to rescue me as an introduction.'

'Aye,' he said; 'funny that. Pity the TV cameras hadn't been there, it would have caused a laugh him going down on the grab,' he nodded towards Bill, 'and the three of us then slithering on our bellies.' He jerked his head at her and paused before saying, 'You should make up a song about that an' all.'

Her eyes widened, but before she could say anything he said, 'Oh, I know quite a lot about you; I thought that song you made up for Duke and them was really fine.'

'You know Duke?'

'We live next door to him in Jarrow.'

'It's a small world.' She shook her head.

'You've said it. By!' he said, 'they're a lot, that group. I don't know why Jimmy strings along with them. Me mother's threatened to get the polis time and time again. They come back from a do on a Saturday night—or a Sunday morning—and start raising the place. Drums, guitars, mouth organs, the lot.'

'You live with your mother?' Her head was bowed enquiringly towards him. 'You're not married?'

For reply he jerked his chin upwards; then running his hand through his hair he said, 'Nearly came off two years ago, but she changed her mind.'

'I'm sorry.'

'Oh, don't be.' He was grinning again. 'She's got a bairn now and she goes about like something the cat dragged in. Talk about counting your blessings; it nearly made me go to church the last time I saw her. . . .'

They were laughing uproariously when the door opened and they both turned and looked at Corny.

Mary Ann got to her feet, saying, 'You've missed it all. This is Johnny Murgatroyd. He . . .'

Corny came forward, saying, 'Jimmy's told me something of

it. It was very good of you.' His voice had a slightly stiff note to it.

Johnny Murgatroyd was on his feet now, his hand extended. 'Oh, that's all right. It was a sort of re-introduction. We know each other; brought up back to back so to speak. I used to chase her when she was a nipper.'

'Oh, yes.' Corny gave a weak smile; then looked from the fellow's coat to his trousers; and Mary Ann said, 'We were covered from head to foot in slime. I've lent him your things. That's all right, isn't it?'

'Oh aye. Yes, yes.' He nodded his head airily; then looking towards the fireplace, he asked, 'How did he get out?'

'Don't ask me; I haven't had time to investigate that yet. But there's one thing certain, it's frightened the life out of him.'

Corny was on his hunkers by the fender and he stroked Bill's back, saying, 'All right old chap?' but Bill made no move towards him.

'He's shivering.' He looked up at Mary Ann.

'I had to wash him and, as I said, he got an awful shock and I think he's still frightened.'

'Well, I'd better be on me way.'

They both turned towards Johnny Murgatroyd. 'If you could give me a sheet of paper to put round my old duds I'd be grateful.' He smiled at Mary Ann and added, 'Then I'll see to somebody taking over from me and dash home and make a change and let you have your things back.' He nodded at Corny now, and Corny said, 'Oh, there's no hurry.'

'Good job we're much of a build.' Johnny's engaging grin widened, and Corny said, 'Aye, it is.' He stared at the man, he was about an inch shorter than himself but of a thicker build and good looking in a sort of way. He was the kind of fellow that women would fall over their feet for.

'Many thanks. I'm grateful.'

'You're welcome,' said Corny.

'I'll pop in again and have a word with you, if that's all right.' He looked at Mary Ann, and Mary Ann resisted looking towards Corny before saying, 'Yes, yes, of course, Johnny.'

Five minutes later, after seeing their visitor away, they returned upstairs, and Mary Ann said, 'You didn't mind me lending him your things?'

'No, no, of course not.'

She stared at him. 'But I couldn't do anything else, he was in such a mess, and I would never have got out of there but for him.'

'Oh, I suppose somebody would have dragged you out. They would have sent down the grab again.'

As he turned away she looked at his back, and then she nipped on her lip to stop herself from smiling and forced herself to say casually, 'Yes, I suppose so, but he seemed the only one who wanted to. It was nice meeting him again after all this time.'

'Yes, yes, very nice I should say.' He was talking from the scullery now. 'And he's going to drop in again. Never waited to be asked. Bit fresh, if you ask me. Going to make you pay for the rescue.'

'Well, that's an attitude to take.' She was looking at him from the doorway as he poured himself out some coffee, and her control went by the board. 'You've got room to talk, haven't you? You can laugh and joke with whom you choose, but because you came in and found me laughing with a man that's all wrong. And after he had done me a great service. I don't think your lady friend has ever done you a service, but then,' she closed her eyes and bobbed her head, 'I may be mistaken.'

She had turned into the kitchen again and like a flash he was after her.

Pulling her round to him, he ground out under his breath, 'Now look you here. We straightened me out last night, now I'm going to straighten you out ... before it goes any further. Johnny Murgatroyd is a womaniser. That is the first time I've met him to speak to, but I've heard quite a lot about him. He was going to be married a while ago but the lass found out he was keeping a woman in Wallsend, and apparently she wasn't the first, and she won't be the last; so Mrs. Boyle, take heed to what I'm saying. No more tête-à-têtes with Mr. Johnny Murgatroyd.'

'You're hurting my shoulders.'

'I'll hurt more than your shoulders if I've got to tell you about this again, I'll skelp your lug for you.'

'Just you try it on.'

'Don't tempt me.'

She watched him stalk from the room; then she sat down on rhe chair near rhe fireplace, and again she was biting on her lip. But now she let the smile spread over her face. It filled her eyes and sank into her being, filling her with a warmth.

A movement to the side of her brought her eyes to Bill. He was on his feet, and slowly stepping over the fender he put his two front paws on her knees and leapt up on to her lap, and there, laying his muzzle between her breasts, he gazed up at her. And she looked back at him. Then after a moment she said to herself, 'Well, well, who would have thought it?' and her arms went round him and she hugged him to her.

CHAPTER SIX

WHAT'S GOOD FOR THE GOOSE

'It is, our David. It is because of the miracle Father Carey made.'

'Don't be daft.'

'I'm not, our David, I'm not daft. I told you I told Father Carey in confession and he said it wanted a miracle, and he made it. Mam was going to throw Bill out. You know she was. She wasn't going to let us keep him, and now she has him all the time and he won't leave her, and she's trainin' him herself. It couldn't have happened if Father Carey hadn't . . .'

They had just got off the bus in Felling and were walking up Stuart Crescent making for Carlisle Street where the school was, and David, jumping into the gutter and kicking at a pebble, said, 'It's 'cos Mam got him out of the hole and he was frightened and she was nice to him, that's why.'

' 'Tisn't. He was frightened of the dark and being tied up and being by hisself. But that didn't make him keep with Mam all the time, like now. You don't believe anything, our David, like you used to. It is a miracle, so!'

David glanced at her and grinned, but she didn't grin back at him. Since he had begun to talk he had moved further and further away from her. At first he had been all for their dad. He was still for their dad; but now he was for other people too, like Jimmy. He was always trailing round after Jimmy. Yet there were odd times when he wanted to be near her, and he would look at her and grin, like he was doing now, and she would feel happy. Only she couldn't feel happy this morning; she had too much on her mind. She said suddenly, 'Do you like Diana Blenkinsop?'

When his reply came with startling suddenness she was in

the gutter beside him. 'You don't? Why?'

David kicked another pebble, then started to dribble it along the roadway. Why didn't he like Diana Blenkinsop? When the answer came to him he turned his head and gave it to Rose Mary: ''Cos me mam doesn't like her.'

'Oh, David.' She was running by his side now. She didn't like Diana Blenkinsop because her dad liked Diana Blenkinsop. And David didn't like Diana Blenkinsop because her mam didn't like Diana Blenkinsop. You see, it was all the same. She said now, 'They were talking about her again last night.'

'I know.' He kept his gaze concentrated on his dribbling feet; the stone veered off into the middle of the road and as he went to follow it Rose Mary grabbed him, crying, 'Eeh no! The cars.' And they returned to the pavement and for a while walked in sedate silence.

When they came in sight of the school gate Rose Mary's step slowed and she said, 'There's that Annabel Morton talkin' to Patricia Gibbs. Patricia promised to bring me a book full of pictures, but she only promised so's she could get you to carry it back.'

David's glance was slanted at her again, his eyebrows showing a surprised lift in their middle, and she nodded at him and said, 'She's gone on you.'

'Polony!'

'It isn't polony, she's sucking up. She wants to be asked to tea, but she's not me best friend and I'm not goin' to.'

Annabel Morton was nearly eight and a big girl for her age, and, as Sarah Flannagan had hated Mary Ann as a child, so Annabel Morton hated Mary Ann's daughter, and the feeling was reciprocated in full. When Annabel's voice, addressing no one in particular, said, 'Somebody stinks.' Rose Mary turned on her like a flash of lightning, crying, 'You! You don't know what you're talking about. Scent doesn't stink, it smells. It's scent, me mam's.'

'It's scent, me mam's,' mimicked Annabel to her solitary listener. 'But it still stinks, doesn't it?'

'You're a pig!' Rose Mary did not yell this statement, she hissed it under her breath and she embroidered it by adding,

79

'If you lift a pig up by its tail its eyes'll drop out. Mind somebody doesn't do that to you.'

This would take some beating, and at the moment Annabel could find nothing with which to match it, and so Rose Mary, having won the first round of the day, put on her swanky walk, which wobbled her buttocks, which in turn swung her short skirt from side to side. The result was entertaining, or annoying; it all depended on the frame of mind of the onlooker....

It was in the middle of the morning, after they had had their milk, that they started to paint. Rose Mary liked the painting lesson, she was good at it. The whole class were doing a mural of history. It was depicting Bonnie Prince Charlie and Flora Macdonald. Each table was doing a section, and then they would put it together and it would fill one wall of the classroom. Rose Mary and Patricia Gibbs and her brother, Tony, were doing the water section with the boat on it. Rose Mary had just mixed up a beautiful deep blue for the water under the boat when Patricia dug her in the ribs with her elbow, at the same time withdrawing from under her painting board a big flat book.

They both looked about the room to ascertain the whereabouts of Miss Plum and saw that they were safe, for she was at the far end showing Cissie Trent what to do. Cissie Trent was dim and took a lot of showing. Patricia quickly flicked over the pages and pointed to a coloured plate and looked at Rose Mary, and Rose Mary looked at the picture. For a moment she couldn't make out what it was. And then she saw it was all about a man and a woman; the woman had hardly anything on the top of her, and the man had long hair right past his shoulders. He was lying on a kind of bed thing and the woman was bending over him with a knife in her hand. Eeh! it looked awful. She looked at Patricia and Patricia looked at her and, her eyes round and bright, she whispered, 'She's going to cut his hair off. It's called Samson and De-lie-la-la.'

'...Sam ... son and De-lie-la-la?' Rose Mary's lips moved widely over the name. 'What's she doing?'

'I told you: she's going to cut his hair off.'

'Eeh! what for?'

'So's he won't be able to do anything.'

80

'What is he going to do?'

'Things.'

'What things? . . . Like what things? Playing a group?'

That explanation was as good as any for Patricia, and she nodded as she smiled, 'Yes. Ah-ha.'

Rose Mary considered a moment before saying, 'But that's daft. How can cutting his hair off stop him playing in a . . . '

They both felt the hot breath on their necks and turned startled eyes towards the face of Annable Morton. But Annabel was looking down at the picture. Then she looked from one to the other, and she said, 'Mushrooms.'

The word was like a sentence of death to both of them. Mushrooms was the word in current use in the classroom to express deep astonishment, amazement or horror. The book was whipped from sight and pushed under Rose Mary's drawing board, and they both attacked their painting with such energy that they were panting when Miss Plum loomed up before them.

'Which of you is hiding a book?'

Patricia looked at Rose Mary, but Rose Mary was staring at Miss Plum.

'Come on. Come on, hand it over.'

Still Rose Mary didn't move.

'Rose Mary! Have you got that book?'

Rose Mary's fingers groped under the pad and she pulled out the book and handed it up to Miss Plum. She had done this without taking her startled gaze from the teacher.

Miss Plum now flicked over the pages of the book, her eyes jerking from one art plate to another, and when her eyes came to rest on Bacchus in his gross nudity sporting with equally bare frolicking females she swallowed deeply; then looking at the children again she said, 'Who owns this book?'

'I do, Miss,' said Patricia.

'Where did you get it?'

'From home, Miss. It's . . . it's me brother's. I took a loan of it.'

Again Miss Plum swallowed, twice this time, before saying, 'When you go home tonight tell your mother, not your brother, that I have this book, Patricia; and tell her I would like to see her. . . . But anyway I will give you a note.'

'Yes, Miss.'

'Now get on with your work, both of you, and I'll deal with you later.'

They both resumed their painting, but with less energy now; and after a while Rose Mary, in a tear-filled voice, whispered, 'You've got me wrong, Patricia Gibbs.'

'Well, you wanted to see it.'

'No I didn't; I didn't ask to see your nasty book.'

' 'Tisn't nasty.'

'Yes, it is. She had no clothes on her . . .' She dare not pronounce the word breast.

' 'Tisn't nasty,' repeated Patricia. 'Our John says it's art. He goes to the art classes at night, he should know.' Her voice sank lower. 'Miss Plum's a nit. . . .'

The result of this little episode was that Rose Mary was met at the gate by Annabel; tactics vary very little with the years. Annabel did what Sarah Flannagan used to do to Mary Ann. She allowed Rose Mary to pass, then fired her dart. 'Dirty pictures,' she said. And when Rose Mary flung round to confront her she repeated loudly and with a defiant thrusting out of her chin, 'DIRTY PICTURES!'

What could one say to this? You couldn't give the answer 'I'm not,' nor could you give the answer 'They weren't,' because in the back of her mind she felt they were.

David was waiting for her at the corner of the railings. He knew all about it, all the class knew about it. Rose Mary thought the whole school knew about it, and soon everybody who went to church would know about it.

She was crying when they got on the bus and their special conductor said, 'Aye, aye! What's this? Got the cane?'

Rose Mary shook her head, then lowered it.

'Well, this is a change; I've never seen you bubbling afore. Something serious happened the day? You set the school on fire?'

Setting the school on fire would have been nothing to the heinous crime for which she was being blamed.

'What's she done?' The conductor was now addressing David pointedly, and David, after glancing at Rose Mary, craned his neck up, indicating that what he had to say must be whispered, and when the conductor put his ear down to him he said, in a voice that was threaded with what might be termed glee, 'She was looking at mucky pictures.'

The conductor's head jerked up. 'Good God! You don't say?'

'I wasn't.' Rose Mary hadn't heard what David had said, but the conductor's reactions told her as plainly as if he had shouted it. She now dug David in the arm with her fist, crying, 'I wasn't, our David.' Then looking up at the conductor, she said, 'I didn't. They were in a book, in Patricia Gibb's book. She was just showing me.'

'Oh!' The conductor was trying hard to keep his face straight. He pushed his cap on to the back of his head and said, 'And the teacher caught you at it?'

Rose Mary nodded.

'Too bad! Too bad!' With his knee he gently nudged David's hip, and this caused David to bow his head and put his hand tightly across his mouth.

Rose Mary was still protesting her innocence not only to the conductor and their David now and the man and woman who were sitting behind them and who were very interested in the tragedy, but also to the two men who were sitting on the other side of the bus.

When she alighted from the bus she imagined that everybody in it suddenly burst out laughing. But then it might only be the funny noise the wheels were making; anyway, she continued to cry and protest at intervals until she reached the house, the kitchen and Mary Ann. . . .

'It's all right. It's all right,' said Mary Ann. 'Now let's get this straight. . . . And you David,' she reached out and pushed David to one side, 'take that grin off your face and stop sniggering, it's nothing to laugh at. Now tell me all about it.' She sat down on the chair and drew Rose Mary on to her knee, and Rose Mary told her and finished, 'I only saw that one, Mam, honest, the one with the man and woman called Sam-son and De-lie-la-la. She hadn't much clothes on and he had long hair, and that was all.'

Mary Ann took a firm hold on her face muscles and forbade

herself to smile. 'Well, now, Samson and De-lie-la- I mean Delilah. She's called Delilah. Say Delilah.'

'De-lie-la-ha.'

'... It's all right. Don't worry, you'll get it. Well, that isn't a dirty picture.'

'It isn't, Mam?'

'No, no; it's a great picture, it's very famous. There's a story about Samson and Delilah.'

So Mary Ann told Rose Mary, and David, the story of Samson and Delilah, and she ended with, 'All his strength was in his hair, you see. Once he was without his hair, Delilah knew that he wouldn't be able to do anything, win battles and things like that, all his strength would go, all his power, and so she cut off his hair.'

'And did it, Mam? I mean, didn't he fight any more battles after, and things?'

'No, no, he didn't.' She didn't go on to explain the gory details of what happened to Samson after this, she left it at that. Instead, she said, 'There, you weren't looking at a mucky picture, you were looking at a great picture. And when you go back to school tomorrow you can tell Annabel Morton that. And if Miss Plum says anything more to you about it you tell her what I've said, that Samson and Delilah is a great picture and there's nothing to be ashamed of in looking at it.'

'Yes, Mam.' Rose Mary's voice was small. She couldn't see herself telling Miss Plum that, but she was comforted nevertheless. And wait until she saw that Annabel Morton, just wait.

'Go on now and get washed and then have your tea. Afterwards you can take Bill out and have a scamper.'

'Has he been out today, Mam?' asked David now, as he rolled Bill on to his back on the mat.

'I took him down the road at dinner-time and left him in the yard a while after, but that's all. He could do with a run. Go on now and get washed, tea's ready.'

They both now ran out of the room, leaving the door open and calling to Bill; and Mary Ann went into the scullery while Bill stood on the mat looking first one way, and then the other, finally he walked towards the scullery.

CHAPTER SEVEN

MATERIAL AND IMAGINATION

The idea came to Mary Ann a fortnight after the incident of
the grab. She sat down, as she usually did after she had finished washing the dinner dishes, with a cup of tea and a book.
Sometimes she gave herself fifteen minutes, sometimes half-an-
hour, it all depended on her interest in what she was reading.
There was no chance to read once the children were home, and
this was the only time of day when there seemed to be an
interval between the chores. But the pattern over the last two
weeks had changed, for as soon as she sat down Bill moved
from the fireplace and took up his position on her lap. She was
amused at the dog's sudden devotion to her, and not at all
displeased, although she still protested to Corny, 'I don't want
the thing up here, but he's quiet and behaving himself—at
least at present, but should he start again . . . well.' And to the
children, when they grumbled, 'He doesn't want to stay out,
Mam; he'll come if you'll come,' she would say, 'Don't be so
silly. Put his lead on and take him over the fields. He's got to
have a run, and I can't take him out all the time. And don't
tug him. And tell him to heel, and sit, and when he does it pat
his head.'

When she talked to them like this they would stare at her in
a disconcerting way and she always had to busy herself in
order not to laugh in front of them, because the transference of
Bill's affection from them to herself was really funny when she
came to think of it. And now here he was on her lap again,
and every time she lifted the book up he would push his
muzzle in front of it and open his mouth and laugh at her.

Mary Ann was convinced that he was laughing; his lolling
tongue, the light in his eyes, the way his dewlaps quivered, he

85

couldn't be doing anything else but laughing.

She had got into the habit over the last few afternoons of talking to him. 'I'd like to read if you don't mind,' she said to him. 'Oh, you do? Well, do you know this is the only time of the day I have to myself? ... What do I want time to myself for? ... Don't ask such a silly question. Oh, you know it's a silly question, do you, and you're sorry.' She put her head on one side and surveyed him; then touching his muzzle with her finger she said, 'You know you are the ugliest thing I've ever seen in my life, at least the ugliest dog, but you've got something.... What? I don't know, you tell me. We've all got something, you say? Oh yes, very likely.... How do you see us, Bill, eh? What do you call us in your mind? Big he, and little she? Angel one, and angel two?'

She laughed at the description of her family and Bill wriggled on her knee, then let his front paws go slack around her hips and placed his muzzle in his favourite position, the hollow of her breasts, and she stroked his head and stared at him, and he stared back at her.

How long they remained like this she wasn't sure but when she next spoke aloud she said, 'It's an idea. Why not? It's worth trying; dafter things than that have been known to succeed. I've seen nothing like it in any of the papers. There's Dorfy of course. She writes dialect pieces in the Shields Gazette, but this would be from a dog's point of view, how he sees us. I could make it funny. Yes, if I tried I could make it funny.... Ooh, I'm sorry.' She had jumped up so quickly that Bill found himself sprawling on the floor and she stooped down and soothed his rumpled feelings. Then looking into his eyes again she said, 'It would be funny, wouldn't it, if it came off.' And now there came into her mind the picture of Diana Blenkinsop.

Diana Blenkinsop, and life from the viewpoint of a dog would appear to have no connection whatever, but in Mary Ann's mind they were closely linked.

During the next three weeks the house was like a simmering kettle, on the point of boiling but never reaching it.

Mary Ann was in a state of suppressed excitement. She was

hugging a secret to herself, and if things worked out, as she prayed they would, that would show them. When her thoughts took this line she saw the picture of Corny and Diana Blenkinsop standing together. Twice in the last week she had seen Diana come out of Corny's office; once she had seen their heads together under the bonnet of her car. She was the type, Mary Ann decided, that would go to any lengths to get what she wanted, even to messing up the engine of her car.

She had written, and written, and re-written three five hundred word snippets about Bill, supposedly his outlook on life, and last Monday she had sent them to the editor of the *Newcastle Courier*. Now the sight of the postman coming along the road would drive her down the stairs to meet him at the door, but here it was Friday and she had received no reply, not even an acknowledgement. But then, she hadn't received the stuff back either, so perhaps no news was good news. . . .

Corny's life over the last three weeks had been one of irritation. First in his mind was the fact that Mary Ann was playing up. She was up to something, he could tell. He only hoped to God it wasn't anything against Diana Blenkinsop, but knowing to what limits she had gone to put things right for her father, one such effort incidentally, resulting in him losing one hand, he was more than a little worried as to what lengths she would go with regards to himself. And then there was Jimmy. For two pins he would give him the sack, but where would he get another like him. Jimmy could turn a car inside out. He was a good worker; give him a job and he stuck at it until it was finished, but the quality didn't make up for being light fingered. Two ten shilling notes had gone from the till this week. The second one he had marked, but when later he had asked Jimmy if he had change for a pound note on him, and Jimmy had given him a ten shilling note and ten shillings worth of silver, it hadn't been the marked note. He was cute was Jimmy; and that was the worst type of thief, a cute one.

And then there was Mr. Blenkinsop. He had come into the garage yesterday and looked around for quite a while before he said, 'You all right, Corny?' and he'd replied, 'Yes, I'm all right. What makes you think I'm not?'

'The little lady all right, Mary Ann?'

'Yes, yes, she's all right.'

Then Mr. Blenkinsop had jerked his head and said 'Oh, I was just wondering.'

He didn't ask him what was making him wonder, he daren't. Had he noticed that his daughter was never away from the garage? Even lunch times now she would come in. She said it was the quickest way to the hill beyond; she sunbathed there when it was fine. She'd even brought her lunch twice or thrice and had it out there. He wished to God she hadn't come to work here. Nothing had been the same since. He was all mixed up inside. He kept telling himself that the next time she put her nose in the door he would ignore her, but when he heard her say 'Cor-ny!' in that particular way she had, he found himself looking at her and smiling at her, and saying, 'Yes. Yes. Yes.' He agreed with every damn thing she said.

But yesterday she had said, 'I wonder what you would be like in a fight, Corny?' and he had said, 'Fight? Who should I fight?'

She had shrugged her shoulders. 'I was just wondering.'

'You don't wonder things like that without a reason.' He had stopped smiling at her, but she had continued to smile at him; then walking away she said, 'Do you know that our handsome ganger is upstairs?'

He made himself utter a small 'Huh!' when she turned and confronted him, then shook his head and said, 'Well, what would you like to make of that? She's known Johnny Murgatroyd since they were bairns.' He had then nodded his head in a cautionary fashion towards her as he said, 'You're a starter, Diana, aren't you?'

'What do you mean, a starter?'

'You know what I mean all right. They could say the same about you. You're in here with me, but you're not going to lose your good name because of that, are you?'

'I might.' She walked a step towards him. 'Perhaps I have already.'

He gulped in his throat, rubbed his hands with an imaginary piece of rag, then said, 'You want your backside smacked, that's what you want. Go on outside and do your sunbathing.'

'You're trying to make me out a child, Cor-ny, aren't you?'

she said. 'But you know I'm not. We both know I'm not, so ...' She tossed her blonde head backwards and her hair jumped from her shoulders as if it was alive. 'We've got to face up to these things. But there's plenty of time, it'll grow on you. I'm in no hurry.'

She went out through the small door in the back wall of the garage, and Corny went to a car, lifted the bonnet and bent over the engine with his hands gripping the framework. My God! What was he to do? She was a little bitch. No, she was a big bitch; a long-legged, beautiful, attractive big bitch. He hated her. No. No, he didn't, he.... His head went further down over the engine. He wouldn't even allow himself to think the word....

And the children? Rose Mary was unhappy for a number of reasons. Their David didn't want to play with her at all. Even when they came home from school he didn't want to play with her like he used to. He would yell at her and say, 'I'm going with the cars.' She didn't want to go into the garage with the cars but she wanted to be near David. And she wanted to be near Bill, but Bill, after ten or fifteen minutes' romping, would make straight for the house and upstairs and their mam. She was glad that Bill liked her mam because now they could keep him. But he just liked her mam and he didn't like her. Well, if he liked her he didn't want to stay with her, he just wanted to stay with her mam. She couldn't understand it.

And then there was her dad. He used to come and play with them when they were in bed. If he was late coming upstairs he would always come into the room and have a game with them. That was, up till lately. Now, even if she kept awake until he came in, he would just kiss her and say good night and God bless, and that was all.

And her mam. Her mam was worried and she knew what her mam was worried about 'cos she had seen her standing to the side of the curtains looking down on to the drive, watching her dad and Diana Blenkinsop. Yet her mam hadn't cried these last few weeks. Of the two, it was her dad she was more worried about. Her dad ... and Diana Blenkinsop....

And David. David, too, had his worries. David's worries were deep; they were things not to be talked about. You didn't think too much about them but you did something to try to get them to go away. His worries were concerned, first with Jimmy, secondly with his dad. About Jimmy he was doing something definite; with regard to the problem of his dad he was working something out.

In a way it was David who had inherited his mother's ingenuity.

CHAPTER EIGHT

BEN

The phone rang about quarter-to-seven. It was Lizzie. 'Is that you, Mary Ann?' she said.

'Yes, Mam.'

'I've got some rather sad news for you. Ben is going fast. Tony's just been down, and he says that Ben asked for you, just as if you were in the house. "Where's Mary Ann?" he said. He's rambling a little, but I wondered whether you'd like to come and see him.'

'Oh, yes, Mam, yes. I didn't know he was ill.'

'He's only been bad since Tuesday. But he's a good age, you know.'

'What's Mr. Lord going to do without him?'

'That's what we're all asking, lass. But he's got Tony and Lettice.'

'I know, I know, but they're not Ben; Ben's been with him nearly all his life.'

'Can you come?'

'Yes, Mam, yes, of course. I was just going to get them ready for bed but Corny will see to them, he's just downstairs.'

'All right, dear. We'll expect you in an hour or so.'

'Bye-bye, Mam.'

'Bye-bye, dear.'

She had put the phone down before she realised that Corny wouldn't be able to run her over, somebody must be here with the children. She could have asked her da to pick her up; but it didn't matter, she'd get the bus.

She ran downstairs and into the office where Corny was sitting at the desk. She forgot for the moment that there was any coldness between them and she said, 'Ben ... Ben's dying.

91

Mam's just phoned, he'd like to see me. Will you put the children to bed?'

He was on his feet looking down at her and he shook his head, saying, 'Aw, poor old Ben. But still he's getting on, it's to be expected.... He asked for you?'

'Mam said so.'

'Well, get yourself away. But look——' He put out his hand towards her and she turned as she was going through the door. 'I won't be able to run you over. Are they coming for you?'

'I forgot to ask Dad.'

'I'll get on to them.'

'No, no, it doesn't matter. He could be busy or anything; I'll get the bus at the corner. If I hurry I'll get the ten past seven.' She was running up the stairs again.

Five minutes later, when she came down, Corny was waiting for her on the drive. 'Get your Dad to bring you back mind.'

'Oh, he'll do that.' She looked up at him. 'Don't let them stay up late, will you?'

'Leave that to me.' He nodded at her.

'And ... and Bill; don't leave him on his own upstairs, will you not? He might start tearing the place up again.'

He smiled wryly at her, then said, 'We couldn't risk that could we?' They stared at each other for a moment; then as she turned away he said to her quietly, 'Forgotten something?' She paused, then looked down at her handbag before saying, 'No I don't think so.'

'Well, if that's how you want it, it's up to you.'

She walked away from him with a quick light step, the only thing about her that was light at the moment.

Whenever they left each other for any length of time she always kissed him, and he her; it might only be a peck on the cheek but it was a symbol that they were close—kind, as Rose Mary would have said.

The sketches she had been writing around Bill during the last three weeks had provided tangents for her thoughts along which to escape from the thing that was filling her mind; the thing that was making her sad deep inside, and not a little fearful. Her impetuous battling character was not coming to her aid over the business of Corny's attraction for Diana Blenkinsop, and no matter what excuse he gave about having to be civil to the girl because of her father she knew it was just an excuse, and she knew that he knew it too. He was attracted to Diana Blenkinsop.

She had always felt she knew more about the workings of a man's mind than she did of a woman's. This was likely, because since she was a small child she had dissected her father's character, sorting out his good points from his bad ones, but loving him all the while. But in her huband's case her reaction to the dissection was different. She had worked and schemed to turn her father's eye and thoughts away from another woman and back to her mother, but she couldn't do that with regard to her husband. She knew that she would never work or scheme to keep Corny, not when there was another woman involved. He would have to stay with her because he loved her, because he found her more attractive than any other woman. He would have to stay with her because her love for him alone would satisfy him. This was one time she could not fight.

She was lost in her thinking and did not notice the car, which had just flashed by, come to a stop until it backed towards her.

'Hello there. Waiting for the bus?'

'Oh, hello, Johnny. Yes, yes, I'm going home; I mean to my mother's.' She still couldn't get out of the habit of thinking of the farm as her home, although Corny had impressed upon her that she had one home now and it was where he lived.

'Get in then; I'll run you along.'

'Oh, no, no, Johnny; the bus will be here in a minute, it's due. I won't take you out of your way.'

'You won't take me out of my way. I'm at a loose end, you'll be doing me a kindness. Come on, get in.'

She stood looking down at him. Corny didn't like this man, he liked him as little as she did Diana Blenkinsop. He'd be wild if he knew she had taken a lift from him, but it seemed silly not to, and he'd get her there in a quarter of the time.

When he leant forward and pushed open the door she could do nothing but slide into the seat beside him. He looked different tonight, very smart, handsome in fact. He was wearing a shirt and tie that the adverts would have described as impeccable, and his light grey suit looked expensive. He had told her that he sometimes picked up fifty pounds a week when bonuses were good. He had been foreman at Quilter's for five years and Bob Quilter thought very highly of him. Johnny wasn't bashful about himself. His car, too, was a good one, and she knew it would take something to run. The way he looked now he had no connection with the ganger on the site.

'Why didn't your hubby run you along?'

When she explained he said, 'Oh, oh, I see.' Then added 'You know, I'll like meeting your mam and dad again. I wonder whether they'll remember me?' He grinned at her.

She had been going to say to him, 'Will you drop me at the end of the road,' but when, in his mind's eye, he was already seeing himself talking to her parents she couldn't do anything else but allow him to drive her up to the farm.

Lizzie was waiting on the lawn for her. She had been expecting to see her hurrying along the road; remembering that the children couldn't be left alone she had phoned the house to say that Mike would come and pick Mary Ann up, but Corny had said she had been gone sometime and would already be on the bus. But here she was getting out of a car with a man.

Mary Ann kissed Lizzie, then said, 'Do you know who this is, Mam?'

Lizzie looked at the man before her. Her face was straight. She shook her head and said, 'Yes, and no. I feel I should know you.'

'Johnny Murgatroyd.'

'Murgatroyd. Oh yes.' Lizzie smiled now. 'Of course, of course. But you've changed somewhat since those days.'

'I ... I told you about him getting me and Bill out of the mud, you remember?'

'Yes, you did. Come in.' Lizzie led the way into the house and Mike got up from his seat and put down his pipe and took Mary Ann in his arms and kissed her; then looking across the big farm kitchen to where the man was standing just inside the door, he said, 'Hello.'

'You don't remember me either?' Johnny came forward.

'Yes, yes, I do, Johnny Murgatroyd.'

94

Johnny turned round and looked from one to the other. 'Recognised at last. No more an orphan. Daddy! Daddy! I've come home.'

They all laughed. 'Oh, you'd take some forgetting.' Mike jerked his head. 'You were a bit of a devil if I remember. How have you come here?' He looked at Mary Ann and Mary Ann said, 'I was waiting for the bus, Da, and . . . and Johnny was passing and he gave me a lift.'

'Oh, I see. Sit down, sit down.'

Johnny Murgatroyd sat down, and he looked at Mike. Mike had said, You'll take some forgetting; well, and so would he. He had a vivid memory of battling, boozing Mike Shaughnessy. Who would have imagined that he would have settled down and had all this? A farm, and a grand house. It's funny how some people fell on their feet. Well, he'd have a grand house one day, just wait and see. Great oaks from little acorns grow.

'Will you have a cup of tea before you go up?' Lizzie was looking at Mary Ann.

'No, Mam; it's no time since I had a meal, I'll go now. But perhaps Johhny here would like one?'

'I never say no to a cuppa.' He was laughing up at Lizzie.

'Thanks for the lift, Johnny, I'll be seeing you.'

'You will. Oh, you will.' He nodded at her, and she went out and through the familiar farmyard and up the hill to the house where lived Mr. Lord, the man who had shaped all their destinies . . . with her help.

She went in the back way as she always did, and it was strange not to see Ben, either in the kitchen or coming from the hall.

Tony met her and kissed her on the cheek. Whenever he did this she was made to wonder how different her life would have been if she had married him as Mr. Lord had schemed she should. But it had been Corny who had filled her horizon since the day she had championed the raggy, tousled-haired individual against Mr. Lord himself. And Tony had married Lettice, a divorcee, and they were both happy, ideally happy. It shone out of their faces whenever she saw them together. And now, as Lettice came towards her, the look was still there, which made her feel a little sad, even a little jealous.

'Hello, my dear,' Lettice kissed her warmly, then asked, 'Are you going into the drawing-room first?'

'Is there time? I mean, how is Ben now?'

'Oh, he's dozing, he keeps waking up at intervals. Just go and say hello first.'

Mr. Lord was sitting, as usual, in his winged chair; during the day he would face the window and look on to the garden, but in the evening he would seat himself to the side of the big open fire.

He did not turn his head when she entered the room. His hands, in characteristic pose, were resting on the arms of the chair, but tonight his chin wasn't up and out, it was bent deep into his chest. She reached him before she said, 'Hello.' She had always greeted him with 'Hello'. He brought his head round to her and a faint light of pleasure came into his pale, watery, blue eyes.

'Hello, my dear,' he said; then he shook his head slowly and said, 'Sad night, sad night.'

'Yes.'

'Sit close to me, here.' He pointed to his knee, and she brought a stool from one side of the fireplace and sat where he had bidden her.

'Part of me will go with him.'

She made no answer to this. She knew it was so.

'A great part.' He stared at her for a moment before he said, 'I have bullied him all his life, shouted, ranted and bullied him, and if we lived for another fifty years together I would continue to do so; it was my way with him. He understood it and never murmured.'

There was a great lump in her throat as she said, 'You were his life, you were all he had and ever wanted; he was never hurt by anything you said or did.'

He moved his head slowly, then said, 'He wasn't a poor man, I'm generous in my way; he could have left me years ago. . . . I wish I had gone before him. But it won't be long anyway before we're together again.'

'Oh.' Her voice broke as she whispered, 'Oh, don't say that. And . . . and it's better this way. If he had been left alone he would have had no one, not really, because there was only you in his life, whereas you've got'—she paused—'all of us.'

He raised his head and looked at her, then put out his long, thin, blue-veined hand and cupped her chin, 'Yes, I've got all of you. But the only one I really ever wanted was you. You know that, child, don't you?'

She was crying openly now and she took his hand and pressed it to her cheek, and he said, 'There, there. Go on, go on up. Twice today he has spoken your name. I know he would like to see you.'

She rose to her feet without further words and went out into the hall. The drawing-room door was open and through it she saw Lettice and Tony standing together. When they turned and saw her they came swiftly to her and Lettice put her arm around her shoulders and said, 'Don't cry, don't upset yourself. Would you like a drink, a sherry, before you go up?'

'No; no, thanks.' Mary Ann wiped her face with her handkerchief, then said, 'I'd better go now.'

'Yes, do,' said Lettice, 'and get it over with, and I'll make some coffee.' She nodded to Tony and he walked up the stairs by Mary Ann's side, and when they entered Ben's room a nurse rose from the side of the bed and, coming towards them, said, 'He's awake.'

Mary Ann went forward and stood gazing down on Ben. He looked a very, very old man, much older than his eighty years. She bent over him and said softly, 'Hello, Ben.'

His thin wrinkled lips moved in a semblance of a smile. Ben had rarely smiled. He had in a way grumbled at others, herself included, as much as his master had grumbled at him. He had never shown any affection towards her. At first he had shown open hostility and jealousy, because from a child she had inveigled herself into his master's good books by being what he considered perky and cheeky, whereas his life-long service elicited nothing but the whiplash of a tongue that was for ever expressing the bitterness of life.

'Mary . . . Mary Ann.'

'Yes, Ben.'

His lips mouthed words that were soundless; then again they moved and he said, 'See to him, he needs you, master needs you.'

'Yes, Ben. Don't worry, I'll see to him.' She did not say that his master had his grandson and his grandson's wife to see to him, for she knew that she, and she alone, could fill the void that Ben would leave in Mr. Lord's life. Even when he had been given a great grandson the boy had not taken her place; and that was very strange when you came to think about it.

'Good girl.'

The tears were flowing down her face again. When she felt the rustle of the nurse's skirt at her side she bent down and kissed the hollow cheek, and Ben closed his eyes.

Tony led her from the room and down the stairs, and in the drawing-room Lettice was waiting, and she said, 'There, sit down and have your coffee.'

'It's ... it's awful. Death is awful.'

'It's got to come to us all,' said Tony solemnly. 'But poor old Ben's done nothing but work all his days, yet we couldn't stop him.'

'He wouldn't have lived to this age if we'd been able to,' said Lettice. 'Work was his life, working for grandad.'

'There aren't many left like him,' said Tony. 'They don't make them any more.'

No, thought Mary Ann, they didn't make Bens any more, not men who were willing to give their lives to others; it was every man for himself these days. The world of Ben and Mr. Lord was passing; it had almost gone. It would vanish entirely, at least from their sphere, when Mr. Lord died, but she prayed that that wouldn't be for a long time yet.

After a while she asked, 'How's Peter?'

'Oh, fine. We had a letter from him this morning,' said Lettice. 'I say fine, but he has his troubles.' She smiled. 'He informs us that he doesn't like the new sports master. His name is Mr. Tollett, and they have nicknamed him Tightrope Tollett. I can't see the connection but likely they can. How are the twins?'

'Oh, they're grand.'

'I hear you've got a dog,' said Tony now, grinning slyly.

'Yes,' said Mary Ann, 'a bull terrier.'

'So I heard. You pick the breeds.'

'I didn't pick him.'

'I understand he created a little disorder in the kitchen.'

'A little disorder is right,' said Mary Ann. 'If I'd had a gun I would have shot him on the spot. Well,' she rose to her feet, 'I'd better be going; I've left Corny to see to them and they play him up.'

'Are you going to look in on grandad again?' asked Lettice.

'Yes, just to say good night. . . .'

Ten minutes later Mary Ann entered the farm kitchen again and stopped just within the door and looked to where Johnny Murgatroyd was still sitting at the table. He called across the room to her, 'You haven't been long.'

As she walked towards her mother she said to him, 'You needn't have waited.'

'Oh, I had nothing better to do.'

'How did you find him?' said Lizzie.

'Very low; they don't think he'll last the night.'

'Poor old Ben,' said Mike. 'He was a good man . . . a good man.' He knocked out the dottle from his pipe on the hob of the fire. 'The old fellow's going to be lost. Things won't be the same.'

Lizzie said now, 'You'll have to pop over and see Mr. Lord more often. In spite of Tony and Lettice he'll miss Ben greatly.'

'Yes,' said Mary Ann, 'I mean to. And now,' she fastened the top button of her coat, 'I'd better get back.'

'Aren't you going to have something to drink?' said Lizzie.

'No; no thanks, Mam, I've just had a cup of coffee with Lettice and Tony.'

As they all went through the hall to the front door Mary Ann said, 'You'll phone me when it happens?'

'Yes, of course, dear,' said Lizzie.

On the drive Johnny held out his hand to Mike, saying, 'Well, it's been nice meeting up with you again, and you, Mrs. S.'

'It's been nice seeing you, Johnny, and talking about old times,' said Lizzie. 'Any time you're passing you must look in.'

'Yes, yes, I will. I won't need another invitation, and don't forget you asked me.'

She laughed at him; then looked at Mary Ann whose face was straight and she said, 'Don't worry, dear.'

As they drove along the lane, Johnny aiming to be sympathetic, said, 'It's a pity about the old fellow but we've all got to go some time. Your dad tells me he's eighty. Well, he's had a good run for his money.'

Mary Ann made no answer to this. Good run for his money. We've all to go some time. All trite expressions meaning nothing. Death was a frightful thing; it was the final of all final things. She knew she shouldn't think like this. Her religion should help her, for wasn't there a life after death, but she couldn't see it. She often thought about death and the fact that it was so final worried her, but it was a thing you couldn't talk about. People didn't want to talk about death. If you talked about death you were classed as morbid. And if you told the priest of your thoughts in confession all you got was you must pray for faith. Lord I believe, help thou my unbelief. At times she got all churned up inside with one thing and another. She thought too much . . . 'What did you say, Johnny?'

'You were miles away. I was saying that I bet you a quid you don't know who I'm taking out the morrow.'

'Now why should I?' she smiled slightly at him. 'I don't know anybody you know.'

'But you do. You know this one all right.'

Her thoughts took her back to Burton Street and the surrounding district. Who did she know there that he knew? The only person who was in her life from that district was Sarah, who was now her sister-in-law. 'You've got me puzzled,' she said; 'I still don't know anyone that you know.'

'Think hard.'

She thought hard, then said, 'I give up.'

'What about Miss Blenkinsop?'

Her surprise lifted her around on the seat and she exclaimed loudly, 'What! You and Diana Blenkinsop? You're joking.'

'No, no, I'm not joking.' His tone was slightly huffed. 'Why should I be joking?' He gave a swift glance at her. 'Because she's the boss's daughter and I'm a ganger? Do I look like a ganger?' He took one hand from the wheel and draped it down the front of himself.

'No, no, I didn't mean that.' But she had meant that.

'I'm going places, Mary Ann.'

'I've no doubt of that, Johnny.' Her smile had widened.

'Do you know something?'

'What?'

'You should be thanking me for telling you, it'll get her out of your hair.'

'What do you mean?' Her body had jerked round again.

'Oh, oh, you know what I mean.'

'I don't.'

'Now, now, Mary Ann, don't let us hide our heads in the sand; you know for a fact that she's got her sights set on your man. Everybody on the job knows it.'

She felt she wanted to be sick, literally sick. She swallowed deeply and took in a great intake of breath before she forced herself to say on an airy note, 'Well, I don't care what they know on the job, it's of no importance. She can have her sights set at any angle, she'll only be wasting her time.'

'Oh, I'm glad you're not worried.'

'I'm not worried.' She sounded cool, confident, and he glanced quickly at her, the corner of his mouth turned upwards. 'Still, I think, me taking her over should help you to be less worried than not being worried, if you get what I mean.'

She remained quiet, thinking. Yes, indeed, this would make her less worried, this would show Corny what kind of girl he was almost going overboard for. The only snag was it couldn't last because when Mr. and Mrs. Blenkinsop got wind of it there'd be an explosion, because beneath all their camaraderie they were snobbish, especially Mrs. Blenkinsop; she kept open house but she vetted the entrants. Mary Ann felt there had been more than a touch of condescension about the invitation that was extended to themselves; it was a sort of boss's wife being nice to an employee's family, attitude. But Corny was no employee of Mr. Blenkinsop.

When they reached the road opposite the garage Corny was serving petrol and he jerked his head up and became quite still

101

as he looked at Mary Ann getting out of the car and the face that was grinning at her from the window. When Johnny Murgatroyd waved to him he made no response but turned and attended to the customer.

A few minutes later he mounted the stairs, telling himself to go carefully.

Mary Ann was in the bedroom with the children and he had to wait a full ten minutes before she came into the kitchen. Her face was not showing sorrow for Ben, nor yet mischievous elation at being driven up to the door by Johnny Murgatroyd; it had a sort of neutral look that took some of the wind out of his sails. He watched her pat Bill and say, 'Down! Down' before he forced himself to say calmly, 'How did you find him?'

'He won't last the night.'

In an ordinary way he would have said, 'I'm sorry about that,' but instead he said, 'Where did you pick that one up?'

She turned and looked at him over her shoulder. 'You mean Johnny?'

'Well, he didn't look like Cliff Michelmore, or Danny Blanchflower, or the Shah of Persia.'

She had a desire to burst out laughing, and she turned her head away and replied coolly, 'I didn't pick him up, he picked me up while I was waiting for the bus.'

He screwed his face up and peered at her back. 'You mean when you were going?'

She turned to him and inclined her head slowly downwards, giving emphasis to his words as she repeated them, 'Yes, when I was going.'

'Then he must have waited for you?'

'Yes, he waited for me, and me dad saw nothing immoral in it; neither did Mam.'

'You mean he took you right to the farm?'

'He took me right to the farm. Isn't it awful, scandalous?' She shook her head in mock horror at herself, and he said quickly, 'Now, you can drop that. And if you've got any sense you'll drop him. And the next time he offers to give you a lift you'll tell him what to do.'

'But perhaps I haven't got any sense, Corny, perhaps I'm like you.'

'Oh, my God!' He put his hand to his brow and turned from her and leaned his shoulder against the mantlepiece. Then pulling himself upwards again he shouted at her, 'Look! I don't let myself be seen around the town in a car with some-one that's notorious, and he is notorious. No decent girl would be seen within a mile of him.'

'Really! you surprise me.'

'I'm warning you.' He took a step forward, his teeth grinding against each other. 'You'd better not go too far.'

Quite suddenly the jocularity was ripped from her tone and she cried back at him. 'You telling me not to go too far! You telling me you wouldn't be seen in the town with anyone like him! No. No, you wouldn't be seen around the town with Miss Blenkinsop because there's no need, you have the privacy of the garage, and the office, haven't you?'

There was a silence that only waited to be shattered, then he cried, 'You're mad, that's what you are, mad. And you'll get what you're asking for.' He marched towards the door, pulled it open, then turned and shouted. 'There'll be nobody but yourself to blame when I walk out. Now remember that. It won't be Diana who has caused it, but you, you and your rotten, jealous mind.'

When the lower door banged the house shook.

In the bedroom the children lay in their bunks perfectly still. Rose Mary was in the bottom bunk and she stared upwards, waiting for David to make a move, and when he didn't she got out of the bunk and, standing on tiptoes, touched his shoulder. But he gave no sign. His face was almost covered by the blanket, and when she pulled it down his eyes were wide open, and they stared at each other.

CHAPTER NINE

ROSE MARY'S SICKNESS

The following morning the postman brought Mary Ann a letter and she wanted to cry, 'Look! look! would you believe it.' It was from the editor of the *Newcastle Courier* and it said simply, 'Dear Mrs. Boyle, I am very interested in your doggy sketches and if you would care to call on me at three o'clock on Monday afternoon we could discuss their publication, subject to alteration and cutting. Yours sincerely, Albert Newman'.

At eleven o'clock her mother phoned to say Ben had died a half-an-hour earlier. She didn't know when the funeral would be, likely about Wednesday, and, of course, she would be going? Yes, said Mary Ann, she'd be there.

'Are you coming over tomorrow?' Lizzie had asked, and Mary Ann answered, 'I think we'll leave it this week, Mam.' There was a long pause before Lizzie had replied 'All right, just as you say.'

Sunday was a long nightmare with Corny working frantically down below in the garage; the children haunting her, not wanting to leave her for a minute, even David; and Bill having another spasm of tearing up everything in sight, until she cried, 'Take him out and keep him out. And keep yourselves out too.'

And they had dragged Bill out and gone into the field behind the house and sat in the derelict car, but they hadn't played.

And so came Monday.

Rose Mary said she felt sick and didn't think she could go to school. 'You're going,' said Mary Ann. She remembered back to the days when she had been so concerned about her father that she had made herself sick and used it as pretence to be off school.

'If she says she's sick, she's sick.' Corny was standing on the landing and he looked through the open door into the bedroom, and Mary Ann looked back at him and said nothing.

'You can't send her to school if she's sick.'

'Very well; she's sick and she needn't go to school.'

Her attitude was infuriating to him, he wanted to break things.

So Rose Mary didn't go to school, but Mary Ann saw that she stayed in bed all morning. She also saw that the enforced inactivity was almost driving her daughter wild, so she allowed her to get up for lunch, and after it, when she asked if she could take Bill out for a walk, Mary Ann said, 'Yes, and tell your father I'm going into town to do some shopping.'

Rose Mary stared at her, her eyes wide.

'Do as I tell you. Take Bill. Put his lead on.'

Bill showed great reluctance, as always, to being moved out of the kitchen, and Mary Ann had to carry him downstairs. Then hurrying back and into the bedroom she made her face up, put on her best suit and hat, looked at herself critically in the mirror, then went out with only a handbag.

Corny noticed this as she crossed the drive; she was carrying no shopping bag and she had on her best clothes. He wanted to dash after her and demand where she was going. He almost called to her, but Jimmy checked him.

'Boss!'

'What is it now?'

Jimmy looked down towards his feet, rubbing his hands together. 'There's something I want to say.'

'Oh, aye.' Corny narrowed his eyes at the young fellow.

'I'm sorry, but ... but ... but I've just got to.'

'Well, whatever it is, you needn't take a week about it. Come on into the office; it's about time you had it off your chest.'

Jimmy's head came up and he stared at his boss striding towards the office, then he followed him. There was nothing much escaped the boss.

'Well, say your piece.' Corny sat himself down on the high

105

stool and looked at the figures in the open book before him, and Jimmy stood just within the door and again he looked down, and now he said, 'I want to give me notice in.'

'What?'

'I'm sorry, boss, but I think it's best.'

'Oh you do, do you? And why do you want to give your notice in?'

'Well, we all need a change now and again.' Jimmy grinned sheepishly.

'More money, I suppose?'

'Aye, more money, boss.'

'You're not getting enough here and not making enough on the side?'

Jimmy stared at him, then said, 'Well the tips are few and far between.'

Corny was on the point of saying, 'Well, I'm not referring to your tips, I'm referring to your light fingers,' but perhaps it was better to let things be this way. He'd never get another like Jimmy for work, but then he'd never get another who would help himself to the takings; he'd see to that before anyone else started. But he couldn't resist one thrust. 'I suppose you've got nearly enough to stand your share in the car by now?'

'Well, not quite, boss, not quite.'

'Oh well, you've still got time, haven't you?' Corny got up from the seat and walked past Jimmy, keeping his eyes on him all the time, and Jimmy returned his stare unblinking. So that was it, he knew. He had known all along.

When Corny reached the drive again his thoughts reverted to Mary Ann. Where was she off to, dressed up like that? Where? WHERE? It couldn't be Murgatroyd. The funeral? No, no, it would be too soon for that. She didn't know yet anyway; and she wouldn't go in that cocky red hat. But perhaps she was going home for something. He would get on to the farm and have a word with Mike, not Lizzie. No; Mike understood things.

Mike answered from the milking parlour. No, Mary Ann wasn't coming there, not to his knowledge.

'What do you think about Johnny Murgatroyd?' Corny

106

asked, and Mike replied 'Johnny? Oh, Johnny's all right. A bit of a lad I understand, but there's no harm in him. Why do you ask? ... Oh, because he brought her home? Oh, don't worry about that, lad. Anyway, as far as I've been able to gather there's only one fellow in her life, and also, I was given to understand, there was only one lass in yours. Does that still hold, Corny?'

'Of course, it does, Mike. I've told you.'

'Is that dame still paying her daily visits?'

There was a pause before Corny said, 'I can't tell her to clear out.'

'You could, you know. And it would clear matters up quicker than a dose of salts.'

'It's easier said than done, Mike.'

'Aye, everything's easier said than done.'

'You have no idea at all where she might be going?'

'Not in the wide world. I'll tap Lizzie, and if I hear anything I'll give you a ring.'

'Don't let on I've phoned you, Mike.'

'No, no; I can keep me big mouth shut when it's necessary. Good-bye, lad, and don't worry.'

'Good-bye, Mike.'

And then he found out where she was, who she was all dolled up for, at least he imagined he had. He was directing the backing of a lorry out of the drive when he heard one of the men on the site shout, 'Where's the boss?' And another, on a laugh, saying, 'Which one?'

'Murgatroyd.'

'Oh, he's gone into Newcastle. A bit of special business I understand.' There was another laugh. 'Swinburne's taken over. He's at yon side of number three shed; they're digging out there.'

This news had an opposite effect on Corny to what might have been expected. His rage seeped away and of a sudden he felt tired and very much alone. He went upstairs and into the kitchen and sat down at the table and, putting his elbows on it, he rested his head in his hands. Well, he had asked for it, and he was getting it. Being Mary Ann she would take nothing lying down. He had threatened to walk out on her but it looked like she wasn't going to give him the chance. How had all this come about? . . .

Rose Mary, in her childish way, was wondering the same thing. Why weren't they all happy like they used to be? Why wasn't everything nice and lovely? The answer was Diana Blenkinsop. She threw the ball for Bill and he fetched it. She threw it again and he fetched it; but the third time she threw it he turned and walked in the direction of the house and she had to run after him and put his lead on.

He was always wanting to be in the house and near her mam. When she had asked for an explanation from her father concerning Bill's change of face he had said that Bill likely felt safer in the house since he had got the fright on the grab, and as it was their mam who had got him out of the whole, he had become attached to her.

She wished she had been the one who had got him out of the hole, and then he wouldn't have wanted to leave her. Everybody was leaving her, their David, and Bill, and now. . . . She wouldn't let her thoughts travel any further along this frightening road. She walked the length of the field, then looked to the top of it where it adjoined the garage, where the men were building the big workshop. As she started up the field someone waved to her from the foot of the scaffolding and after a moment she waved back.

Then she was away, dashing up the field, dragging Bill with her.

'Hello, Rose Mary.' Mr. Blenkinsop looked down on her as she stood panting. 'Why aren't you at school?'

'I was sick and couldn't go.'

'Oh, I'm sorry to hear that. Are you better now?'

'Yes, thank you.'

'Eating too many sweets I suppose?' He bent down to her, smiling into her face, but she didn't smile back as she said, 'No, I didn't have any sweets, I didn't want any.'

He straightened up and surveyed her for a moment. This wasn't the Rose Mary Boyle that he had come to know. He was well schooled in childish ailments, and the look on her face wasn't derived from a tummy upset, if he was any judge. Tummy upsets were soon forgotten when children got out into

108

the open air, especially with a dog. He'd had a feeling recently that things weren't as harmonious as they might be in the little house above the garage. He began to walk away from the building and down the field, and Rose Mary walked with him. Mr. Blenkinsop knew it wasn't good tactics to quiz children, but very often it was the only way anyone could get information. He said, 'I haven't seen your mother for days, how is she?'

There was a pause before Rose Mary answered, 'Not very well. She's gone into Newcastle; she's got her best things on.'

She looked up at him and he looked down at her again, and she answered the question in his eyes by saying. 'She doesn't put her best things on except for something special.'

He nodded his head slowly at her. 'And what's this special thing your mother's gone into Newcastle for ... with her best things on?' He nodded his head slowly at her.

'I don't know.'

'You don't know?'

'No, and me dad doesn't know. She just said for me to tell him that she was going shopping and she didn't take a basket, and she never goes shopping in her best things.'

They had stopped and were holding each other's gaze. 'You have no idea why she went into Newcastle?' He bent his head slightly downwards now and she answered, 'I think I have.'

'Can you tell me?' His voice was very low.

'It's ... it's because me dad's going to leave us.'

He straightened up, his shoulders back, his chin tucked into his neck, and it was a full minute before he said, 'Your dad ... your father's going to leave you?'

'He said he was on Friday night.'

He gave a little laugh now, then drew in a long breath before exclaiming, 'O ... h! mothers and fathers always argue and have little fights and say they're going to leave each other, but they never do. I shouldn't worry.'

'Mr. Blenkinsop.'

'Yes, what is it?' He was bending over her again, his face full of sympathy, and he watched her lips moving around the words 'Would you' like a deaf-mute straining to talk. It wasn't until he said, 'Tell me. Come along, you can tell me what's troubling you. I won't tell anyone, I promise,' that she startled him by saying, 'Would ... would you send your Diana away, please?'

He was standing straight again, his eyes screwed up. His mind was working furiously; a voice inside him was bawling 'No, no, this can't be.' Yet in an odd way he knew, he had known it all along. But he said to her quietly, 'Why do you want me to send Diana away, Rose Mary?'

'Because ...' She closed her eyes now and bent her head.

'Come on, tell me.' He put his fingers under her chin and raised her head, and she said, 'Because she's going to take me dad away.'

'God Almighty!' It was a deep oath. If she'd broken up this happy family, he'd break her neck; as much as he loved her he'd break her neck. She was like her mother. How could women be such devils. And how could men love them for being devils.

He knew that all good-looking men were a challenge to his wife and must be brought to her feet, but once there she let them go. Some of them, he remembered with shame for her, had crawled away broken. Time had taught him to understand his wife; for her to be entirely happy she must have these little diversions, these diversions that kept her ego balanced. She had said to him, 'At heart I'm a one man woman, and men are fools if they can't see that. It's up to them.'

Diana had had boys fluttering round her since she was ten. She had already been engaged and broken it off, but she had never tried, as far as he knew anyway, to capture a married man. Boyle was a big, attractive-looking fellow in his way, an honest fellow too. It was his honesty that had decided his cousin, Rodney, to build the plant on this side of the spare land. He was no empty-headed fool was young Boyle, but on the other hand he was the type that if he reached Diana's feet and she kicked him, he'd break. Self-esteem would see to that.

Well, whatever he had to do, he must do it warily, for his daughter, he knew, was as headstrong as an unbroken colt, and a jerk on the reins at this stage might send her off, dragging Boyle with her.

He put his hand on Rose Mary's head and, bringing his face

close to hers, said, 'Now you're not to worry any more. Do you hear me? Everything's going to be all right.'

'You'll send her away?'

'I don't know what I'm going to do yet. This is just between you and me. You won't tell anyone will you what you've told me?'

'Oh, no. But our David knows.'

'He does?'

'Yes.'

'But he doesn't know that you were going to tell me?'

'Oh, no.'

'Well then, you go on home, and remember not a word to anybody. Not even to David. Promise?'

'Promise.' She made a cross on the yoke of her dress somewhere in the region of her heart and he patted her head again and said, 'Go on now.' And she turned from him, Bill pulling her into a run as she went towards home. And Mr. Blenkinsop walked slowly up the field towards the building, and again he said deep, in his throat, 'God Almighty!'

CHAPTER TEN

FAME AND FORTUNE

Meanwhile Mary Ann was in Newcastle sitting in an office opposite a small bald-headed man. Mr. Newman was smiling broadly at Mary Ann as he said, 'I have found them very refreshing, very amusing, something different.'

'Thank you.'

'Have you done much of this kind of thing?'

'I've been scribbling all my life but I've never had anything published.'

'Well, it's about time you did, isn't it?'

She smiled back at him and said, 'You're very kind.'

'Oh, we can't afford to be kind in this business, Mrs. Boyle. If work hasn't merit it doesn't get published on sympathy, or because,' he poked his head forward, 'you happen to know the editor.'

They were laughing.

'Have you any more of these ready?'

'I've got another three.' She opened her bag and handed him an envelope, and he said, 'Good. Good,' and as he pulled the scripts out he added, 'The main thing is will you be able to keep up this kind of humour; you know humorous stuff is the most difficult to write.'

'It's always come easy to me. Well, what I mean is, I can write something funny where I could never write an essay or descriptive stuff.'

'You never know what you can do until you try. By the way, I was thinking that it would be a good idea just to sign these articles "Bill", no name or anything. You see they're supposed to be written by him. Well, what do you think about that?'

What did she think about it? Not much. It was half the

pleasure, all the pleasure in fact to see one's name in print, and, let's face it, for other people to see your name in print.

He said on a thin laugh, 'I know how you feel about this, but take my advice and let them be written by Bill, the bull terrier, and they'll likely catch on, much more so than if they were written by Mrs. Mary Boyle.'

'Mary Ann Boyle.'

He inclined his head towards her, 'Mrs. Mary Ann Boyle. Well, you see?'

Yes, she saw, and she smiled back at him.

'I like the way you started the first one. It got me reading straight away.' He picked up one of the scripts from the table and read:

"There is a tide in the affairs of men which, taken at the flood, leads on to fortune. So said some fellow. And there is a day in the span of a dog which decides what kind of dog's life he's going to have.

'Most kids know to some extent where they'll be for the first few years, but a dog knows, as soon as he stops sucking out he goes, so naturally he goes on sucking as long as the skin of his belly will stand it. I did, I was the biggest sucker in the business.'

He looked across at Mary Ann and said, 'It's fresh. I mean fresh, you know which kind?'

'Yes, yes, I know which kind.' She was laughing again.

He turned over a couple of pages and pointed, saying, 'This bit where you bring him home and he names you all: Big he, Little she, Angel one and Angel two. Where did you get the idea from?'

'Oh, it was the day he got hung up on the grab and the craneman dropped him into the hole. You know, it's in the third one.'

'Oh yes, I had a good laugh over that one. I passed it on to my assistant and he said you had a wonderful imagination.'

She shook her head slowly. 'It actually happened, just as I put it down.'

'You're joking?'

113

'No, no, I'm not.'

'And from hating his guts you took to him as it says here?'

'Yes, that's how it happened.'

'And you mean to say the one about him getting you up in the middle of the night and then finding the place in shreds in the morning is true?'

'Yes, honest, everything.'

'Well, well, but nobody will believe it. This Bill must be a lad.'

'He is, but since the business of the grab he won't leave me. And the second one, that one you've got in your hand,' she pointed, 'that's about him getting into our bed in the middle of the night, and Corny, my husband, waking up and finding a black wet muzzle an inch from his face; if it had been a hand grenade he couldn't have moved faster. Poor Bill didn't know what had hit him.'

Mr. Newman was laughing again, then he said, 'I may have to tighten things up here and there, do you mind?'

'No, not at all. I'm only too pleased that you like them.'

'Oh, I like them all right. I only hope that they catch on. You can never tell. I aim to print one each Saturday for a few weeks. It would be very nice if the younger generation scrambled for the paper to find out what Bill had been up to during the week, wouldn't it?'

She shook her head slowly. 'It would be marvellous.'

'Well, now, down to basic facts. How about ten guineas.'

'Ten guineas?' Her brows puckered slightly, and at this he said, 'For each publication,' and as her face cleared he laughed and added, 'Oh, we're not as bad as that.'

'I'd be very grateful for ten guineas.'

He rose to his feet and, holding out his hand, said, 'Let's hope this is the beginning of a long and successful series concerning one Bill, a bull terrier.'

'I hope so, too. . . .'

When she was outside she walked in a daze until she reached the bottom of Northumberland Street, and there she thought, I'll phone him and tell him. She knew it would be better this way, because under the circumstances she couldn't go back and look at him and say 'I'm going to do a series for *The Courier*,'

114

not with this other thing between them. And also, on the phone she wouldn't see his face, or witness his reactions, and so there was a chance she would remain calm.

When she heard his voice she said, 'It's me, Corny.'

'Oh!'

'I'm ... I'm in Newcastle.'

'So you're in Newcastle!'

She closed her eyes. 'I ... I thought I would phone you, I've something to tell you.'

There was a short silence, and then his voice came rasping at her, 'Oh, you have, have you? And you haven't the courage to face me. Whose idea was it that you should phone it? Is he holding your hand ... breathing down your neck?' The last was almost a yell and she took the earphone away from her face and stared at it in utter perplexity for a moment, until his voice came at her again, louder now, 'If you're there, Mr. Murgatroyd, let me tell you this....'

She didn't hear his next words for his voice was so loud it blurred the line and she mouthed to herself, 'Murgatroyd! Murgatroyd! He must be barmy.'

When the line became silent again she said, 'Are you finished?' and the answer she got was, 'Go to hell!'

When she heard the receiver being banged down she leant against the wall of the kiosk. Well, if she wanted her own back she was certainly getting it. But she didn't want her own back, not in this way.

It was as she was passing the station on the way to the bus terminus that a lorry drew up alongside the kerb and a voice hailed her, 'Hi, there!'

When she turned round and saw Johnny's grinning face looking down at her she said aloud, 'Oh, no! No!'

'You going back home?'

She ran across the pavement and to the door of the cab and, looking up at him, she said, 'Yes I'm going back but not with you.'

'What's up?' His face was straight.

'Nothing. Nothing.'

'There must be something for you to jump the gun like that. I haven't asked you to go back with me, but I was going to.'

115

The grin almost reappeared and then, getting down from the cab, he said, 'What is it?'

'Look, Johnny, just leave me and get back.'

'No, no, I'm not going back.' He thrust his hands into his pockets. 'I want to know what's up. It concerns me doesn't it?'

'Look, Johnny, it's like this,' she said breathlessly. 'I came in this afternoon to meet the editor of the *Newcastle Courier* and I didn't tell Corny because, well, well we had a bit of a row. But just a minute ago I phoned him and,' she put her hand up to her brow, 'he nearly bawled my head off; he ... he thinks I'm here with you.'

'Huh! you're kiddin'. What gave him that idea?'

'You know as much as I do about that.'

'He must be do-lally.'

'I think we're all going do-lally.'

He laughed at her now. 'All right,' he said. 'I wouldn't embarrass you for the world ... Mrs. Boyle. I'll tell you what I'll do. I'll go straight to the garage when I get back and ...'

'Oh, no! No!'

'Now look.' He lifted his hand and patted her shoulder gently. 'Leave this to me. I'm the soul of tact. I am. I am. I'll do it innocently; I'll tell him exactly what I came into New-castle for, it's in the back there.' He pointed to an odd-shaped piece of machinery in the lorry. 'I'll do it when he's filling me up. I'll ask after you and the children and when you get home he'll be eating out of your hand. Now go and have a cup of tea. Don't get the next bus, give me time.'

'Oh, Johnny.' Her shoulders drooped. 'What a mess!'

'We all find ourselves in it some time or other. The only consolation I can offer you is you're not alone. Go on now, have a cuppa. Be seeing you.' He pulled himself up into the cab and she walked away and did as he advised and went into a café and had a cup of tea.

Corny didn't exactly eat out of her hand when she arrived home. He looked at her as she crossed the drive going towards the front door, then turned away, and it was a full fifteen minutes before he came upstairs and stood inside the kitchen

116

with his back to the door and watched her as she stood cutting bread at the side table. After gulping deep in his throat he muttered, 'I'm sorry about this afternoon.'

She didn't move, nor speak, but when she felt him standing behind her she began to tremble.

'I'm sorry I went on like that.'

Still she didn't answer. She piled the bread on the plate now and when she went to move away he touched her lightly on the arm, saying quietly, 'What was it you wanted to tell me?'

'Nothing.'

'Come on now.' He pulled her round to him, but she held the plate in both hands, and it kept them apart.

'You didn't get dressed up and go into Newcastle and then go into a phone box and call me for nothing. I said I'm sorry. In a way . . . well, you should be glad I'm jealous of him.'

She didn't speak or look at him as he took the plate from her hands and put it on the table, but when he went to put his arms around her she drew back from him, and his brows gathered and his teeth met tightly for a moment. But he forced himself to repeat quietly, 'Come on, tell me what it is.'

She looked at him now and, her voice cool, she said, 'I've had some articles accepted by *The Courier*. The editor asked to see them this afternoon.'

'You have?' His expression was one of surprise and pleasure and he repeated, 'You have. And by *The Courier*! Lord, that's a good start. Well, well.' He nodded his head to her. 'I've told you all along you'd do it. And to get into *The Courier* is something. By, I'd say it is. What are they about?'

'Bill.'

'What!' His cheeks were pushing his eyes into deep hollows; his whole face was screwed up with astonishment. 'Bill? You've written articles on Bill?'

'Yes, on Bill.'

'What about?'

'Oh!' She turned to the table. 'Just the things he does.'

'Well I never!' His voice sounded a little flat now. 'Are they funny like?'

'You'll have to judge for yourself when you read them.'

'I will. Yes,' he nodded at her again, 'I'll read them after tea. By the way, what are they giving you?'

'Ten guineas.'

'Each?' His voice was high.

'Yes,' she paused, then added, 'He's got six. If they take on I'll be doing them every week.'

Into the silence that now fell on them Jimmy's voice came from the bottom of the stairs, calling, 'Are you there, boss?' and when Corny went on to the landing Jimmy looked up at him and said, 'Bloke's asking for you.'

'All right, I'll be down.' Corny looked back towards the kitchen but he didn't return to it; he went slowly down the stairs, and at the bottom he paused for a moment. Ten guineas a time. It would make her feel independent of him. He didn't like it, he didn't like it at all. It was a thing he had about money. He never wanted her to have anything in that line but what he provided.

CHAPTER ELEVEN

THE WILL

Ben was buried on Wednesday. It was the first time Mary Ann had been to a cremation, and although the disposal seemed more final than burying, there was a greater sense of peace about the whole thing than if they had stood round an open grave. She'd always had a horror of graves and coffins, but this way of going was clean somehow.

As the curtains glided on silent rails and covered up the last move Ben's earthly body was to experience, she fancied she saw him young again. Yet she had never even seen a picture of Ben when he was young. His back had been bent the first time she had clapped eyes on him when he had opened the door to her that morning in the far, far past, the morning she had gone in search of ... 'the Lord' to beg him to give her da a job. It was Ben who had tried to throw her out of the house; it was Ben who had been jealous of her; but it was Ben who had, in his own strange way, come to depend on her because he realised that through her, and only her, would his master know life again.

She walked with Corny out of the little chapel. They followed behind Tony and Lettice. Then came her mother and father, and Michael and Sarah. Sarah always came last so that her shambling walk would not impede others. Mr. Lord was not at the funeral, it would have been too much for him.

Tony, looking at Mary Ann, now said, 'Will you come back to the house?'

'If you don't mind, Tony, I'd rather go home. I'll——'

'He asked for you. There's a will to be read and he asked us all to be there.'

She glanced at Corny but his look was non-committal. It

said, 'it's up to you.'

'It won't take long.' It was Mike speaking to her now. 'And you could do with a cup of tea. There's nothing to rush for anyway. The children will be all right with Jimmy when they get back from school.'

When they reached the house they took their coats off in the hall, then filed into the drawing-room. The day was very warm, almost like a June day, not one in early September, but Mr. Lord was sitting close to the fire.

Mary Ann went straight to him. She did not, as usual, say, 'Hello,' nor did he speak to her, but when she put her hand on his he took it and held it gently, and she sat down by his side.

When they were all seated Lettice served the tea that the daily woman had brought in; then she tried, with the help of Tony, to make conversation, but found it rather difficult with Mr. Lord sitting silent, and Mary Ann having little to say either.

It was almost twenty minutes later when the trolley removed, Mr. Lord looked at Tony and said, 'Will you bring me that letter from the desk?' And when the letter was in his hand he looked at it, then at the assembled company and said, 'This is Ben's will. I don't know what it holds, only that it wasn't drawn up by a solicitor. He wrote it out himself about five or six years ago and had it witnessed by my gardener and his wife, then he put it into my keeping, and he didn't mention it from that day.' He paused and swallowed and his Adam's apple sent ripples down the loose skin of his neck. 'I will get my grandson to read it to you. Whatever it holds, his wishes will be carried out to the letter.'

Tony split the long envelope open with a paper knife, then drew out a single foolscap sheet, and after unfolding it he scanned the heading, then looked from one to the other before he began to read. 'This is my last will and testament and I make it on the first day of December, nineteen hundred and sixty-two. My estate is invested in three building societies and up to date the total is nine thousand three hundred and twenty-five pounds, and God willing it may grow. I'm in my right

120

mind and I wish to dispose of it as follows: I wish to leave one thousand pounds to Peter Brown, my master's great-grandson. This to be kept in trust for him until the age of sixteen, because at sixteen I think a boy needs a lot of things, which are mostly not good for him, at least so he is told, but by the age of twenty-one when it appears right and proper he should have these things very often the taste for them has gone.

'When I say I leave nothing to my young master, Mr. Tony Brown, I am sure he will understand, because he has all he needs and more. To his wife, Madam Lettice, I leave my grateful thanks for the kindness and consideration she has shewn me since she has become mistress of this house. Never did I think I could tolerate a woman running my master's house but I found that my young master's wife was an exception.

'To my master, I leave the memory of my utter devotion. There has been no one in my life for fifty-two years other than himself; he knows this.

'To Michael Shaughnessy, farmer on my master's estate, I leave the sum of three hundred pounds because here was a man big enough and bold enough to overcome the dirty deals life has a habit of dealing out.'

At this point Tony raised his eyes and smiled towards Mike, and Mike, his eyes wide, his lips apart, his head moving slightly, looked back at him in amazement. Then Tony resumed his reading.

'Now I come to the main recipient of my estate, namely Mary Ann Shaughnessy. Although she is now Mrs. Mary Ann Boyle I still think of her as Mary Ann Shaughnessy. After the above commitments have been met I wish her to have whatever is left. I do this because, when, as a loving, cheeky, fearless child, she came into my master's life, he became alive again. She turned him from an embittered man, upon whom I, with all my devotion, was unable to make any impression, into a human being once more. You will forgive me, Master, for stating this so plainly, but you and I know it to be true. It was this child, this Mary Ann Shaughnessy, who melted the ice around your heart.

'There is another reason, Mary Ann, why I want you to have and enjoy the money I have worked for, but which brought me no comfort, no pleasure. It is because right from the first you were kind to me, and concerned for me, even when you feared me, so I . . .'

Tony's words were cut off by the sound of choked, painful sobbing. Mary Ann was bent forward, her face buried in her hands.

'There now, there now.' Lizzie was at one side of her and Lettice at the other. The men were on their feet, with the exception of Mr. Lord. Mr. Lord's face was turned towards the fire and his jaw bones showed white under his blue-veined skin.

Lettice now led Mary Ann into her room and there Mary Ann dropped on to the couch, her face still covered with her hands, and her sobbing increased until it racked her whole body.

When Corny came to her side he put his hands on her shoulders and, shaking her gently, said, 'Come on now, give over, stop it.' But his attention only seemed to make her worse.

Now Tony came on the scene. He had a glass in his hand and, bending over the back of the couch, he coaxed her: 'Come on. Come on, dear, drink this.'

But Mary Ann continued to sob and he handed the glass to Lizzie, saying, 'Make her drink it; I must get back to grandfather, he's upset.'

'Mary Ann, stop it! Do you hear?' Corny had pushed Lizzie aside almost roughly and was once more gripping Mary Ann's shoulders, and Lizzie, her voice steely now, said, 'Don't Corny, don't. Let her cry it out. She needs to cry.' She looked at him full in the face, then more gently she said, 'Leave her for a while, she'll be all right.'

He straightened up and stared at her, at this woman who had never wanted him for her daughter. They had always been good friends, but he often wondered what went on under Lizzie's poised and tactful exterior.

He walked slowly out of the room and closed the door behind him, and when he looked across the wide hall there was Mike standing at the bottom of the stairs, his elbow resting on

122

the balustrade. Corny went up to him and Mike said, 'It was the shock; it was a shock to me an' all. Three hundred pounds!' He shook his head slowly. 'Fancy old Ben thinking of me.' Then taking a deep breath he added, 'This is going to make a difference, isn't it? It's a small fortune she's got. Nearly eight thousand pounds I should imagine by the time it's all worked out. Of course, there'll be death duties to pay.' He stared at Corny now. 'You don't look very happy about it, lad.'

Corny stared back at Mike. He could speak the truth to his father-in-law; they were brothers under the skin. He said bluntly, 'No, I'm not happy about it. What do you think it'll do to her?'

'Do to her? Well, knowing Mary Ann, not much.'

'Huh!' Corny tossed his head. 'You think so? Well I see it differently.'

'What do you mean?'

'Oh, nothing.' He brought his shoulders hunching up cupping his head. The action looked as if he was retreating from something, and Mike said, 'Don't be daft, man; money will make no difference to Mary Ann. You should know that.'

Corny turned slowly towards him and quietly he asked him, 'How would you have felt if it had been left to Lizzie?'

Mike opened his mouth to speak, then closed it again. Aye, how would he have felt if it had been left to Lizzie? It would have made her independent of him. It didn't do for a woman to have money, at least not more than the man she was married to. He stared back into Corny's eyes and said, 'Aye, I see what you mean.'

CHAPTER TWELVE

SAMSON AGAIN

On the Thursday night, David leant over his bunk and, looking down on to Rose Mary, whispered, 'We could cut it off.'

'What?' she whispered back at him.

'Her hair.'

'Whose?'

'Don't be goofy, you know whose, Diana Blenkinsop's.'

Rose Mary was sitting bolt upright now, her face only inches from her brother's hanging upside down in mid air, and she said, 'Eeh! our David, that's wicked. Whatever gave you that idea?'

'Mam.'

'Mam?'

'Yes, 'bout Samson.'

'Samson?'

'Don't be so mutton-nappered. You remember, she told us the story about Samson. When he had his hair cut off he couldn't do nothin'.'

'But Samson was a man.'

'It's all the same. And she would look different with her hair off, all like that.' He took one hand from the edge of the bunk and traced his finger in a jagged line around his neck, and Rose Mary exclaimed on a horrified note, 'Eeh! you dursen't.'

'I dare.'

And as she stared at him she knew he dared.

'They're still not kind,' he said.

'I asked Mr. Blenkinsop to send her away.'

David swung himself down from the bunk and, crouching on the floor at her side, exclaimed incredulously, 'When?'

'Last Monday, when I pretended I was sick,' She crimped her face at him. 'I only wanted to stay off so I could see Mr. Blenkinsop.'

'And what did he say?'

'He said I hadn't to worry; he would see to it.'

'Well, he hasn't, has he?'

She shook her head slowly, and he stared back at her through the dim light, looking deep into her eyes and appealing to her to solve this problem, as he had been wont to do, but inarticulately, before he could speak; and she answered the look in his eyes by whispering very low, 'I'll die if she takes me dad away.'

As he continued to stare at her, his mind registered the death-like process they would go through if Diana Blenkinsop did take their dad away. At the end of his thinking he added to himself, And Jimmy and all. But he comforted himself on this point. Jimmy wouldn't go; he could stop that, he would see to that the morrow.

Rose Mary broke into his thoughts now, saying, 'But you couldn't reach.'

'If the sun's shining and it's hot like it was the day, she'll go down and lie on the bank sun bathing. She lies with her hair all out at the back. The men on the scaffolding were watchin' her the day, and laughin'.'

'But you've got to go to school.'

'I could have a headache.'

Again they were staring at each other. Then Rose Mary whispered, 'But me mam won't stand for me being off again, I can't say I'm sick again.'

'I'll do it on me own.'

'Eeh! no, our David, I should be with you.'

'I'll be all right.' He nodded at her. 'If it's sunny in the mornin' I'll say me head's bad.'

The door opening suddenly brought both their heads towards the light and their mother.

'What are you doing out of bed?'

'I've ... I've got a bad head.'

'You didn't say anything about a bad head when you came to bed. Go on, get up.' She hoisted him up into the bunk, then tucked the clothes around him and said, 'Go to sleep and your headache will be gone when you wake up.' Then she tucked Rose Mary in again and, going towards the door, said, 'Now no more talking. Get yourselves to sleep.'

Back in the living-room she sat down near the fire. Bill was lying on the mat, and when he rose and went to climb on to her knee she said, 'No, no!' But he stood with his front paws on her lap looking at her and again she said, 'No!' and on this he dropped his heavy body down and lay by the side of her chair.

There was a magazine lying on the little table to the side of her. She picked it up, then put it down again. She couldn't read, she couldn't settle to anything. She felt that she was moving into a world of delirium. She still wanted to cry when she thought of Ben and what he had done for her, but she mustn't start that again.

Last night she had cried until she fell asleep, and this morning she had felt terrible; and the feeling wasn't caused by her crying alone but by Corny's attitude to this great slice of luck that had befallen her. He wasn't pleased that Ben had left her the money, in fact he was angry. She had wanted to say to him, 'But we'll share it, we've shared everything'; yet she didn't because they weren't sharing everything as of old. She couldn't share even the surface of his affection with Diana Blenkinsop.

The odd thing about the money was that she hadn't brought up the subject to him, or he to her. She had hardly seen him since this morning. He had come up to dinner and eaten it in silence and then had gone straight down again. The same had happened at teatime. And now it was almost nine o'clock and he was still downstairs. He would have to come up some time and he'd have to talk about it some time.

It was half-an-hour later when he entered the room. She had his supper ready on the table and she said to him, 'Tea or coffee?'

'Tea,' he answered.

That was all, just 'Tea'. When she had made the tea and they were seated at the table she said quietly, 'Tony phoned. He ... he wants me to go to Newcastle on Monday to see the bank manager and Mr. Lord's solicitor.'

126

He had a piece of cold ham poised before his mouth when, turning his head slightly towards her, he said flatly, 'Well, what about it?'

'O . . . oh!' She was on her feet, her hands gripping the edge of the table. 'You're wild, aren't you? You're wild because Ben left me that money.'

He put the ham in his mouth and chewed on it before he replied grimly, 'The word isn't wild, I just think it's a mistake you being left it. It was hard enough living with you before, but God knows what it'll be like now with fame and fortune hitting you at one go.'

Her face slowly stretched in amazement as she looked at him and she repeated, 'What did you say?'

'You heard me.'

'Yes, I heard you. It was hard enough living with me before. Well! well! now I'm learning something. Hard enough living with me. . . .' Her voice rose almost to a squeak.

'Yes, yes, it was if you want to know, because for years I've had to contend with your home. This was never your home, as I've told you before. This was just a little shack that I provided for you, it wasn't home, you never referred to it as home. But the farm was home, wasn't it? Then your mother never wanting me to have you, because I was just a mechanic, and she's never let me forget it.'

'Oh! Corny Boyle. How can you sit there and spit out such lies. Mam's been wonderful to you; she's been . . .'

'Oh yes, she's been wonderful to me, like Tony has, the great Mr. Lord's grandson, the man you should have married, the man your mother wanted you to marry, the man Mr. Lord created for you. Aye, created.' He raised his hand high in the air. 'And did he not prepare you for such an elevated station by sending you to a convent and giving you big ideas. . . . Oh aye, they're all wonderful.'

Mary Ann stepped back from the table still keeping her eyes on him. She had never imagined for a moment he thought like this, but all these things must have been fermenting in his mind for years.

He had stopped his eating and was staring down at his plate, and she had the urge to run to him and put her arms about him

127

and say 'Oh, you silly billy! You're jealous, and you haven't got one real reason in the world to be jealous of me. As for the money, take the lot, put it in the business, do what you like with it, it doesn't matter. What matters is that everything should be all right between us, that we should be . . . kind.' But she smothered the urge; nothing had changed, there was still Diana Blenkinsop.

She turned away and went into the kitchen and stood looking out of the small window and watched the lights of the cars flashing by on the main road half a mile away.

After a while she heard him pushing his chair back, and then his voice came from the scullery door, saying, 'I'm sorry. You enjoy your money. Take the holiday you've always been on about. I'm off to bed, I'm tired.'

She made no response by word or movement. He had said he was sorry in a voice that was still full of bitterness. 'Take a holiday,' he had said. Well, perhaps she would do that. She would take the children and go away some place. It would give him time to think and sort himself out. On the other hand it might give him time to throw himself into the waiting arms of Diana Blenkinsop. Well, if that's what he wanted then he must have it. She could see no greater purgatory in life than living with someone who didn't really want you.

CHAPTER THIRTEEN

MR. BLENKINSOP'S STRATEGY

On Friday morning Mr. Blenkinsop arrived at the office not at nine o'clock, but nearer ten, because he hadn't come from Newcastle, where he stayed during the week, but from his home in Doncaster.

Last night, unknown to his daughter, he had returned home because he wanted to talk to his wife privately, and urgently.

During the journey he had rehearsed what he was going to say to her. He would begin with: 'Now look here, Ida, you've been against her going to America.' And doubtless she would come back at him immediately and he would let her have her say because he, too, hadn't taken to the idea when his cousin, Rodney, first suggested that Diana should go out to Detroit. The idea was that mixing business with pleasure she would take up a post in the factory out there with a view to coming back and acting as manageress over the women's department. Recently, however, he had changed his views about this matter and had put it to his wife that it might be a good thing for their daughter to have this experience. But Ida wouldn't hear of it. The family would be broken up soon enough, she had protested; she wasn't going to force any member to leave it.

Yet how would she react when she learnt that the member in question could be preparing to fly from the nest at any moment. He wasn't considering Corny's power of resistance, because few men, he imagined, could resist anyone as luscious as his daughter, especially a man who had been married for seven or eight years. It was a crucial time in marriage; there was a great deal of truth in the seven year itch. Moreover, he knew that when Diana set her mind on anything she would have it, even if when she got it she smashed it into smithereens, as she had done with many a toy she had craved for as a child. Now her toys were men.

But when Mr. Blenkinsop reached home he found his wife knew all about the business. At least that was the impression he got as soon as he entered the house. She was entertaining three friends to tea. From the drawing-room window she had seen him getting out of his car on the drive and had met him in the hall, saying rapidly under her breath, 'I expected you. Say nothing about it though when you come in; Florence and Kate are here. Jessie Reeves popped in unexpectedly. I'm wondering if she knows anything; Kate gave me a funny look when she came in. The Reeveses were out Chalford way on Sunday too. They might have seen them, but say nothing.' She turned from him and led the way back into the drawing-room and, a little mystified, he followed her.

Chalford! it wasn't likely Boyle took her to Chalford on Sunday.

He greeted the three ladies, talked with them, joked with them and half-an-hour later saw them to their cars. Yet again he was obstructed from having any private conversation with his wife by his family descending on him and demanding to know what had brought them back on a Thursday night.

'It's my house. I can come back any time I like.' He pushed at the boys' heads, hugged Susan to him, then demanded to know what was happening to their homework; and eventually he returned to the drawing-room and closed the door. Looking at his wife he let out a long slow breath and said, 'Well!'

'Yes, indeed.' Ida Blenkinsop draped one arm over the head of the couch and lifted her slim legs up on to it before adding, 'You can exclaim, well! Of all the people she could take up with! When I think of her turning her nose up at Reg Foster, and Brian, and Charles. And look what Charles will be one of these days, he's nearly reached three thousand now. The trouble with this one is, he looks all right, too all right I understand, but what he'll sound like is another thing, and how he'll act is yet another.'

Dan Blenkinsop stood with his back to the fire, his hands in his pockets, looking at his wife. He was puzzled and becoming more puzzled every moment. He said now, 'How did you get to know?'

'Well, Kate ran into them on Sunday. She thought nothing of it; they were on the bridge looking at the water near Chalford. She saw them getting into this big car and thought, Oh! But then on Wednesday she was with John in Newcastle and there they met them again, and John recognised the fellow. He says he is well over thirty and a womaniser. He worked on a building in Newcastle that John designed. . . .'

'What! Look, Ida.' Dan screwed up his eyes and flapped his hand in front of his face in an effort to check her flow. 'Look, stop a minute and tell me who you're talking about.'

'Who I'm talking about?' She swung her legs off the couch. 'Diana, of course, and your ganger.'

'My ganger?' He stepped off the Chinese hearthrug and moved towards her, his chin thrust out enquiringly, and he repeated, 'My ganger?'

'Yes, a man called Murgatroyd. John Murgatroyd.'

There was a chair near the head of the couch and Dan lowered himself on to it; then bending towards his wife he said, 'You mean that Diana's going out with Murgatroyd, the ganger?'

'What do you think I've been talking about. And'—she spread out her hands widely—'what's brought you back tonight? I thought that's what you'd come about.'

Dan took his handkerchief from his pocket and wiped his brow.

'It wasn't that?'

He now looked up under his lids at his wife and said slowly, 'It was about Diana, but not with Murgatroyd. You mean to say she's been going out with Johnny Murgatroyd?'

'You know him?' She shook her head. 'Of course you know him; what am I talking about? But what is he like? He's just an ordinary workman isn't he? And why have you come if not about that. Is anything else wrong?'

Again he mopped his brow as he said patiently, 'Not wrong; I would say a little complicated. I came out tonight, dear, to suggest that it would be as well if you changed your mind about her going to America. You know she wanted to go, but

131

you were so dead against it she allowed herself to be persuaded.'

'Now don't rub it in, Dan.' Ida Blenkinsop turned her face away, and her husband said quickly, 'I'm not rubbing it in, but I think it would be the best thing under the circumstances, because I've got something else to tell you.'

Her face was towards him again, her eyes wide with enquiry.

'She's causing havoc in the Boyle family.'

'You mean with him . . . Corny?'

'Yes, with him, Corny.'

'You're joking. That's as bad as the ganger.'

'It might appear so on the surface. To my mind it's much worse. The ganger happens to be single; Corny's got a wife and two children, and even the children are aware of the situation.'

'Oh Dan!' She had risen to her feet. 'You're exaggerating.' Her tone was airy.

Dan now got to his feet and, his voice patient no longer, he snapped, 'I'm not exaggerating, Ida, and I'm really concerned, not for our daughter but for the Boyle family. I tell you the children know. That little girl came to me, and you know what she said? She asked me if I would send Diana away because she didn't want to lose her daddy.'

'Good gracious! I've never heard of such a thing. That's precociousness. She's like her mother that child. . . .'

'Ida! you've got to face up to this. If Diana doesn't go haywire with Boyle she'll go it with Murgatroyd. But I want to see that she doesn't go it with young Boyle. That's a nice family and I would never forgive myself if she broke it up. But I know what you're thinking. Oh, yes I do. You would rather she amused herself in that direction than go for Murgatroyd, because you think she's safe with Boyle, him being married, whereas she could get tied up with . . . the ganger, and then you'd have to bury your head in the sand. Now from tomorrow night I'm going to tell her she's finished down there at the factory. I'm going to tell her I've heard from Rodney and he's renewed his invitation for her to go out to him. I'm going to

132

get through to Rodney tonight and explain things, and there'll be a letter for her from him early next week endorsing all I've said.'

Ida Blenkinsop put her hand up to her cheek and walked across the room to the window, where she stood for a few minutes before coming back. Then looking at her husband she said, 'What if she meets a Boyle or a Murgatroyd out there?'

'We'll have to take our chance on that. But there's one thing I'm determined on, she's not going to break up the Boyle family to afford herself a little amusement, and as long as she's within walking distance of him, or driving distance for that matter, she'll see him as a challenge.'

'It's his wife's fault.' Ida Blenkinsop jerked her chin to the side. 'She should look after her man and see that he doesn't stray. Little women are all alike; they're all tongue and no talent. I could never stand little women, not really.'

As he took her arm and smiled at her and said, 'Come on, let's have something to eat, I'm hungry,' he was thinking: And neither can your daughter, for he now sensed that Diana's hunting of Corny was as much to vex his wife as to satisfy her craving for male adulation.

It was about twenty past ten on the Friday morning when Mr. Blenkinsop came into the garage. Corny was at the far door and when he saw him he felt the muscles of his stomach tense. Diana had left the garage only a few minutes earlier. He had been in the pit under the car and he had caught sight of her legs first, long, slim, brown ... and bare. She was wearing a mini skirt but he couldn't see the bottom of it, only the length of her legs.

When she bent down and her face came on a level with his he couldn't look at it for a moment, yet when he looked away his eyes were drawn to her thighs, which were partly exposed and within inches of his hands.

'Good morning.' That was all she had said but she could make it sound like the opening bars of an overture. She was wearing a scent that wiped out the smell of the petrol and oil. She looked fresh, young, and beautiful, so beautiful that he ached as he looked at her. He wetted his lips and said, 'Hello, there.'

'Busy?'

'No, this is a new form of exercise; they say it prevents you from getting old.'

She laughed softly. 'You're the type that'll never grow old, Corny.'

'Nice of you to say so, but you see before you a man literally prone with age.'

She laughed softly. 'When you feel like that it's a sure sign you need a change.'

'I'm inclined to agree with you.'

'It's a beautiful day.'

'I hadn't really noticed, not until a minute ago.' He wasn't used to paying compliments and the thought that he had done so brought the blood rushing to his face, but when she laughed out loud he knew a moment's fear in case the sound carried upwards and into the house.

'Do you know something?'

'What?'

'You're very, very nice, Mr. Cornelius Boyle.'

He lowered his eyes for a moment, looked at the spanner in his right hand, moved his lips outwards, then drew them in tight between his teeth before he replied, 'And you know something?'

'What?'

'You are more than nice, Miss Diana Blenkinsop, much, much more than nice.' He dare not allow himself to look into her eyes; his gaze was fixed on her hair where it fell over her shoulders and rested on the points of her small breasts.

'Dad! Dad! where's Jimmy?'

He blinked quickly, his body jerked as if he had been dreaming and, turning his head, he looked at the face of his son peering at him from yon side of the car, and he said, 'He . . . he's about somewhere. In . . . in the yard, I think.'

David did not say 'All right, Dad', and run off; he still knelt on the edge of the well, his head inclined to one shoulder, and he gazed at his dad then at the other face beyond his dad.

'Well, I must be off. I'm looking for Father. He hasn't

134

turned up yet; I thought he might be wandering around the works.'

'I haven't seen him.'

Her face became still; her eyes looked into his. 'We'll meet again.' Her smile showed all her teeth, like a telly advert. When her face lifted from his he watched her body unfold, he watched her legs as they walked away, then he turned again slowly on to his back and lay gasping for a moment.

What was going to be the outcome of it? They were nearing some point of revelation. He knew it and she knew it. Dear God, what was he going to do? Mary Ann. Oh, Mary Ann. He wanted help. He thought of Mike, but Mike could do nothing more. There was no alternative only his own reserves, and God knew they were pretty weak at the moment.

'Dad!'

He had forgotten about David and he turned his head towards him, saying, 'You still there, what do you want?'

'Can I help you?'

'No, no. I thought you had a bad head?'

'I have.'

'Well, go out in the fresh air.'

'Yes, Dad.'

After David moved away he lay until he felt his stomach heaving as if he were going to be sick, and he crawled from under the car and went to the back gate and took in great draughts of fresh air. As she said, it was a beautiful morning, like a summer's day; the world was bright, she was bright and beautiful and young, so young. . . . Mary Ann was young, yet Mary Ann was like a child compared with her, because Diana had knowledge that Mary Ann had no notion of. Diana had a knowledge of men, what they wanted, what they needed. She was like a woman made out of history, all the Salome's, all the Cleopatra's, all the essence of all the women who had made love their business.

It was as he turned into the garage again that he saw Mr. Blenkinsop at the far door.

'Hello, there. Can I have a word with you, Corny?'

Mr. Blenkinsop was looking at him in an odd way and the sweat began to run down from his oxters and soak his shirt.

'Yes, yes,' he nodded his head quickly. 'Would you like to come into the office?' He led the way into his office and there he said, 'Take a seat.'

Mr. Blenkinsop sat down on the only chair, but Corny did not perch himself on the high stool but stood with his back to his desk and pressed his hips against it as if for support, and as he looked at Mr. Blenkinsop's bent head his sweating increased, and he ran a finger round the neck of his overalls. Then Mr. Blenkinsop raised his head and said, 'I don't like to probe into a man's private life but this is one time when I'm forced to. I want to ask you what you know about Johnny Murgatroyd?'

The question came as such a surprise that Corny gaped for a moment, then said, 'Johnny? Johnny Murgatroyd?'

'Yes.'

'Well, as you say, a man's private life is his own, but one hears things. What has he been up to?'

'It's not what he's been up to but what he might be up to.' The words were slow and meaningful, yet Corny didn't get the gist of them until a thought struck him. Was he trying to tell him something about Mary Ann and Murgatroyd? The thought brought him from the desk and he stretched himself upwards before he said, 'What do you want to say, Mr. Blenkinsop?'

'Well, it's rather a delicate matter, Corny. I . . .'

Corny felt himself bridling. He'd say it was a delicate matter; and what damn business was it of his anyway. He said stiffly, 'My wife's known Jimmy Murgatroyd since they were children together. They lived next door to each other so to speak.'

'Oh, I didn't know that, but one hears things you know. Do you think there's any truth in the rumour that he's had a number of women, not girls, women, if you follow me?'

'Yes, I follow you.' Corny nodded at him slowly. 'But as I said, and as you said, the man's life's his own, it's nobody's business except his and those concerned.'

'Quite right, quite right.' Mr. Blenkinsop made a movement that expressed his understanding, and then he said, 'I agree with you, a man's life is his own and he can do what he likes

136

with it, until it impinges on your daughter's life and then one sees it differently.'

Corny had been standing straight, almost rigid, and now he brought his head down. It moved lower and lower and his eyes held Mr. Blenkinsop's for a full minute before he said, 'Murgatroyd and Diana?'

'Yes, Murgatroyd and Diana.'

Now his shoulders were moving upwards again, taking his head with them, and he made a sound like a laugh as he said, 'No, no, you've been listening to rumours, Mr. Blenkinsop. Diana going with Murgatroyd? Never!'

The laughing sound he made increased. There was an assurance about it until Mr. Blenkinsop, getting to his feet, said, 'I haven't been listening to rumours, Corny; I only wish I had. She's going around with him. She was at a dance last Saturday night with him. I went to the house where she is staying. They're very nice people, he calls for her there. She was out with him all day on Sunday and she didn't get back until turned one o'clock on Monday morning. She's seen him every night this week and has never been in before twelve. Mrs. Foster, the woman she's staying with, was glad I called. She's been a little worried, not because she knows anything against Murgatroyd but because she thinks he's too old for her and,' he pursed his lips, 'not quite her class.'

Corny was leaning against the edge of the desk again. He was staring down at his feet. Again he was feeling sick but it was a different kind of sickness now. It was a sickness bred of shame, self-recrimination, and the feeling that only a man gets when he knows he's been made a fool of, when he's been taken for a ride, a long, long ride; when he's been used, laughed at.

Johnny Murgatroyd, the scum of the earth. And where sex was concerned he was the scum of the earth. Her father had said that she was out with him until one o'clock in the morning. Well, no one could be out with a man like Johnny Murgatroyd and not know what it was all about. Oh, God! He was so sick, sick to the core of him. And not ten minutes ago she had looked into his eyes and promised him anything he had in mind to ask. Or had she? Had it just been his imagination?

137

NO. NO. It had not been his imagination. He had been neither drunk nor daft these past weeks, but one thing he had been, and that was besotted by a cheap sexy slut.

Mr. Blenkinsop had been talking for some minutes and he hadn't heard him and he brought his attention back to him again to hear him say, 'Rodney wanted her to go to America and I think the only way to nip this in the bud is to send her packing, so to speak. Of course, her mother and I will miss her terribly but we can't stand by and let her ruin her life. And you know young girls are very headstrong; when they get it into their head they're in love they imagine they'll die if they don't get their way. Yet with a girl like Diana she'll be in and out of love, if I know anything, for a good many years to come.... I hope you didn't mind me asking about Murgatroyd, but if there's nothing you really know against him, well, that's that.'

Corny found his voice to say, 'I only know he's unmarried and women seem to like him.'

'Oh yes, yes.' Mr. Blenkinsop was walking out of the office now and he smiled over his shoulder at Corny and said, 'There's no doubt about that. He's a very, very presentable man, but I don't want him,' his voice dropped and he repeated, 'I don't want him for a son-in-law, you understand?'

Corny understood. He also hoped in this moment that Mr. Blenkinsop would get him for a son-in-law. He hoped that Murgatroyd would in some way manage to marry Diana Blenkinsop, and by God it would serve her right.

'Well, I must get off now, but thanks, Corny. You really don't mind me having asked you about him?'

'Oh no, not at all.'

'Thanks. Good-bye.'

'Good-bye, Mr. Blenkinsop.'

He returned to the office, and now he did sit on his stool and he supported his slumped shoulders by crossing his arms on the desk. And in this moment he felt so low, so belittled there was no hole so small that he couldn't have crawled into.

Mary Ann opened the sideboard drawer and took out a pair of binoculars. They had originally been used by some naval man but now looked very much the worse for wear. She had picked them up in a second-hand shop about two years ago, around the time that Corny was taking an interest in bird life to while away the time between passing motorists. He had said to her one day, 'You wouldn't believe it but I've seen ten different kinds of birds on the spare land this morning. I couldn't make out half of them, only to see that they were different. You can't get near enough to them. What you want are field glasses when looking at birds.'

She had said, 'I'll get you a book on the different types of birds; you can get them in that small series.' She hadn't thought about the glasses until she had seen them lying among some junk in a dirty-looking shop in a back street in New-castle. She had been amazed that she had been asked three pounds for them, but she had paid it, and Corny had had a lot of fun out of the glasses. That was until the stroke of luck came, and he had never touched the glasses since. But she had. She had used these glasses day after day over the past weeks, round about dinnertime, because it was at dinnertime that Diana Blenkinsop sauntered over the spare land. When it was fine she had her lunch out there on the knoll; even when it was raining she would saunter down the field, past the derelict old car that the children played with, down to where the land rose to form the knoll, and where, Mary Ann knew, the men, as they sat munching their bait, would be able to see her plainly standing silhouetted against the sky.

As time went on it was a compelling urge that made her take up the field glasses. She always seemed to know the time when the figure would appear from the side of the half-erected car park. This sprang from the same instinct that told her when Diana Blenkinsop was down in the garage. She seemed to be able to smell her there. The feeling would bring her to a stop in the middle of some job and carry her to the front room, to the side of the window, and as sure as life a few minutes later she would see the tall, lithe figure sauntering across the drive.

She stood now to the side of the scullery window and lifted the glasses to her eyes. Yes, there she was already ensconced, and she must have had her lunch because she was sunbathing.

She was lying spreadeagled like a body being sacrificed to the sun.

She was brazen, utterly brazen. Mary Ann's lips tightened. She looked all legs, bare legs. Oh, men! Couldn't Corny see what she was?

Her attention was now brought from the knoll to the derelict car and the figure that had just emerged from the shelter of it. It was David. When she realised that her son was going towards Diana Blenkinsop there entered into her a deeper note of bitterness. Even children were attracted to her. Not Rose Mary. No. No female would be. When she saw David drop on to the ground she screwed up her eyes and re-focused the glasses. What on earth was he doing? He was crawling, up the side of the knoll, right behind the prone figure.

What ... on ... earth ... was he up to? Perhaps he was playing a game? He was going to give her a fright.

When he was within less than an arm's length of Diana Blenkinsop she saw him stop, and then her heart almost ceased to beat when his hand, holding something in it from which the sun glinted as if from steel, moved towards the head lying on the grass.

She gripped the glasses tightly to her face as she cried, 'David! David! Don't! Don't!' The next minute she saw Diana Blenkinsop spring to her feet and hold her head. Then David turned and ran down the hill, and Diana after him.

Now she herself was flying down the back stairs, through the yard and on to the open space behind the garage, there to see Diana Blenkinsop belabouring David about the head and shoulders.

No tigress could have covered the distance quicker and, tearing her son from the enraged girl, she cried, 'You! You great big useless hussy, take that!'

She'd had to reach up some distance to deliver the blow, but such was its force that it made Diana Blenkinsop reel backwards and she stood for a moment cupping her face before she cried, 'How dare you! HOW DARE YOU!'

'You say how dare I? You have the nerve to say how dare I? And you beating my son?'

'Beating your son?' Diana Blenkinsop was spitting the

140

words at Mary Ann now. 'Yes, and I'll beat him again. Just look. See what's he's done.' She lifted the front of her hair to show a jagged line about six inches from the bottom and two inches in width. 'He was cutting my hair off, the horrible little tyke.' She was glaring down at David, and David, from the shelter of his mother's waist, slanted his eyes up to her and clung tighter to Mary Ann.

'Whatever he did, you've got no right to lay hands on him; you should have come to me.'

'Come to you!' The words held deep scorn. 'And what would you have done? You can't control any member of your family from your dog upwards. Your children take no more notice of you than your husband does.'

Mary Ann found difficulty in breathing, and her words came as a hissed whisper through her trembling lips. 'You cheap, loose individual, you!'

There was a slight pause before Diana said, 'You had better be careful, but whatever I am, I can lay no claim to commonness.' Her lip curled on the word. 'There's a difference, Mrs. Boyle.'

At this point she raised her eyes from Mary Ann's face to the small garage door and her head wagged slightly as she watched Corny come and stand beside his wife. He was looking at her as he had never looked at her before and he said quietly, 'Yes as you say, Diana, there is a difference between cheap and common, yet some folks can be both.'

As Diana stared into the face that was almost on a level with her own, she knew that her power over this man was gone. He had likely heard about Johnny. Oh well, what did it matter. The sea was teeming with such fish. She said to him, 'Your son tried to cut my hair off.'

Corny cast a swift glance down at David; then looking back at her, he said, 'Did he now!'

'Yes, he did now.' She mimicked his inflexion, then added, 'And your wife struck me.'

'Oh, she did, did she?' Now he looked down at Mary Ann. But Mary Ann did not return his glance; she was staring at the girl, sensing something had happened, even before this incident, between her and Corny.

141

'Yes, she did. She's keeping true to type, the back street type.'

Corny took a step from Mary Ann's side as he said grimly, 'I'll have you remember it's my wife you're talking about.'

'Oh, la-la! Aren't we becoming loyal all of a sudden! You must have lost your amnesia. How does it feel to remember you've got a wife?'

Corny's arms were stiff by his sides, his muscles tense, his finger nails digging into his palms. He was getting all he had asked for, and more. God, how could he have been so blind! Could it be that just over an hour ago there was some part of him that had loved this hussy. Aye, he'd have to admit it, some part of him had loved her; not in the way he loved Mary Ann but in a way that was like a craving for drugs, or drink. And now there was nobody in the wide world he hated as he did her.

He watched her coming nearer to him, her eyes fixed scornfully on his. She passed him without a word, but when she came to Mary Ann she paused slightly, and looking down at her, said, 'I should give him back his trousers, it might help him to find out whether he's a man or not.'

Mary Ann was in front of him, hanging on to his upraised arm. The trembling of his body went through hers. She did not look up at his face but kept her eyes fixed on the arm she was holding, yet she knew that he was watching the figure moving towards the small door in the garage. When she felt he could see her no longer she released her hold, but still not looking at him she said under her breath, 'You'd better come upstairs ... and you an' all.' She put out her hand and pulled David towards her, and with him by her side she walked slowly forward. But she had covered more than half of the open space before she heard the crunch of Corny's steps behind her.

In the kitchen she was glad to sit down; every bone in her body was shaking. She did not know whether it was with anger or relief; anger at the things that girl had said, or relief at the knowledge that whatever had been between her and Corny was finished, dead.

When she saw Corny enter the room, she bowed her head

142

against the look on his face. The thing might be dead but she felt he was suffering the loss as if of a beloved one.... It wasn't over yet then.

She had to do something to ease the embarrassment between them so she pulled David towards her, and, her voice trembling, she asked him, 'Tell me, what made you do it?'

David stood before her with his head bent. When he raised his eyes he didn't look at her, but at his father who was standing with his elbows resting on the mantelpiece, his back towards them, and he said, 'Because of Samson.'

'Samson!' Mary Ann gazed at her son in perplexity. Then she asked, 'Which Samson?'

'The Samson you told me and Rose Mary about with the long hair.'

Mary Ann shook her head slightly and waited.

'Well, you said that when his hair was cut he couldn't do anything, he was no use. You said everything was in his hair, an' I thought'—he glanced quickly at his father's back again, then ended on a high cracked note, 'I thought she couldn't do anything if her hair ...'

When his voice broke he screwed up his eyes tightly and the tears welled from between his lashes, and Mary Ann drew him into her arms and held him for a moment. Then rising from her chair, she took him by the hand and into the bathroom, and before she washed his face she held him again, and kissed him and murmured over him, 'Oh David. David.' And he cried now with his eyes open and whispered, 'He won't go, will he, Mam? Dad won't go?' And she whispered back, 'No, no. Don't worry; you've made it all right.'

Whether he had or not, at least he had been the means of proving to her that Diana Blenkinsop was gone. But the question now was, had her effect on Corny been such that their life, as it had once been, was a thing so dead that it could never be revived?

CHAPTER FOURTEEN

THE ETHICS OF STEALING

It was just after three o'clock when David approached Jimmy for the second time that day. 'Are you still busy?' he said to him.

'Aye,' said Jimmy, without looking at him.

'I told you I've got somethin' to show you.'

'And I told you I don't want to see it.'

David stood looking at Jimmy's bent body; he was cleaning an engine that was jacked upon a low platform.

'It won't take five minutes, Jimmy.'

'I told you I haven't got five minutes. And what if your dad comes and finds me away from my job?' He straightened up and looked down on the small boy, and David looked back at him and said, 'But you're goin' the night.'

'Aye, I'm goin' the night, and a bloomin' good job an' all.'

David now turned from him and went to the door of the shed and looked into the yard, then coming back he whispered, 'Will you not go away until I come back, I mean into the garage, I've got something for you?'

'I'll be here for the next half hour or so,' said Jimmy flatly.

Jimmy watched the boy run out of the shed and across the yard, and he shook his head and muttered to himself, 'Who would believe it, eh, who would believe it?'

In less than five minutes David was back in the shed, and when he closed the door Jimmy shouted at him, 'Leave that open, I want to see.'

'Just for a minute, Jimmy. I'll switch the light on.'

He now came and stood in front of Jimmy. He was holding in his hands a cocoa tin with a lid on it and he held it out, saying, 'It's for you, for the car, so you won't have to go.'

144

Jimmy bent his thin bony body over David and he said one word, 'Eh?'

'You wanted money for the car, for your share. I haven't got it all but there's a lot, and me pocket money an' all. I only kept sixpence back of me pocket money and put the other one and six in.'

'Chree-ist!' exclaimed Jimmy. 'Don't tell me you've been taking it for me?' He was showing not only his teeth but his gums, and his face looked comical, but he didn't feel comical. He knew the kid had been pinching for weeks now and he knew that when the boss twigged the money was missing he would get the blame of it. He had wanted to tip the boss the wink, but he found he couldn't. How could you tell him his own bairn was a thief? He couldn't do it, he liked the boss. The only thing he could do was to leave and let him find out for himself. The boss was always easy with money, and he had been very easy these past few months when it had been flooding in, and he himself could have made quite a bit on the side but he wasn't given that way. But he would never have guessed in a month of Sundays that the young 'un was taking it for him, for the car. He remembered the day Poodle Patter had come into the garage and tried to persuade him to go to Baxter's. The kid had been listening then. Crikey! what was he to do now? He dropped on to an upturned wooden box and, looking at David, said, 'Aw man, you're daft, barmy, clean barmy.'

With the change in Jimmy's attitude David's face brightened and he pulled the lid off the tin and emptied the contents on to the bench. There were ten shilling notes, pound notes, and one five-pound note.

Jimmy closed his eyes, then put his hand over them, and when he heard David say excitedly, 'There's nearly ten pounds. You won't have to go now, will you?' he looked at the boy and said slowly, 'David man, don't you know you've been stealin'? Don't you know you'll get something for your corner for this.'

'It isn't lock-up stealing, Jimmy, not real stealing, it's just from Dad, and he's got lots of money, and he doesn't bother about change, you know he doesn't. He said, "What's six-pence?"'

'Aye, he might have said what's sixpence, man, but look, these are not just sixpences, there's a fiver. When, in the name of God, did you take that?'

'Just a while back.'

'Oh crikey!'

'You won't go now, Jimmy, will you?'

Jimmy looked down into the round face that was wearing an almost angelic expression and he was lost for words. This here kid was a corker. You never knew what he was going to get up to next, but to pinch for him! It put a different complexion on the whole thing. He'd have to do something about it.

He gathered up the money and put it back into the tin and, gazing down at David, he said, 'Now look; I've got a little job I want you to do for me. Now will you stay here and do it until I come back?'

'Aye, Jimmy, I'll do it for you, but,' he paused, 'you won't leave, will you?'

Jimmy looked back into the now solemn countenance, and he jerked his head and rubbed his lips with his tongue before saying, 'We'll see. We'll see. Only you stick at this job. Now take that bit of glass paper and get a polish on this rod. I want to see me face in it. Right?'

'Right, Jimmy.'

Corny was in the office. The till was open and he was look-ing at the contents. He slanted his eyes towards Jimmy as he stood at the door but he didn't speak, and Jimmy said, 'Could I have a word with you, boss?'

Still Corny didn't answer. There was a five-pound note missing from the till. He wanted to turn on this lad and say, 'Hand it over before I knock it out of you!' but in another hour or so he would be gone and that would be that. And, by damn, he'd see that the new one who was starting on Monday didn't grease his fingers at his expense.

Jimmy didn't know how to begin, and the boss wasn't being very helpful. He looked in a bit of a stew. Well that to-do at dinnertime with that piece and the missus was enough to put anybody in a stew, but he didn't think the missus would be troubled any more by Miss Blenkinsop, and that was a good thing. He had been sorry for the missus lately, and he couldn't for the life of him understand the boss. He said now, 'There was a reason, boss, why I wanted to leave.'

'I've no doubt about that.' Corny's voice was cold.

Coo! he was in a stew. And now having to tell him what his lad had been up to was a bit thick, but there was no other way out of it. 'You ... I don't know whether you've noticed anything about the takings, boss, but ... but there's been money going.'

Corny slid from the stool and stared at Jimmy and he said, 'Aye, aye, Jimmy, there's been money going. But it's rather late in the day isn't it to give me an explanation?'

As Jimmy stared back into Corny's eyes, he realised the thing he had feared, the thing he was leaving for had already happened; the boss had known about it all along and thought it was him. Aw, crikey! He wagged his head from side to side, then thrusting the tin towards Corny, he said, 'It's all in there. But ... but it wasn't me that took it.'

Corny looked at the cocoa tin, then lifted the lid. Following this he turned out the contents on to the desk and picked up the five-pound note. Slowly now he turned round and looked at Jimmy, then he said, 'Well, if you didn't take it, who did? The fairies? There's only you and me dealing with money here.'

Jimmy bowed his head. 'You remember Poodle Patter coming and tryin' to get me to go a share in the car for the band, boss?'

Corny made no response and Jimmy went on, 'He was at me to go to Baxter's for more money, and to get rid of him I said I would think about it. Well, there was somebody listening and they thought up a way to get the money for me.' He lifted his head and looked at Corny and said simply, 'Young David.'

Corny stared at him. He stared and he continued to stare until Jimmy said, 'I'm sorry, boss.'

'Our David!' It was a mere whisper, and Jimmy nodded his head once. 'You mean he's been stealing from the——' he thumbed the till, 'all this time, under my nose?'

Jimmy said nothing until Corny asked, 'How long have you

147

known about this?'

'Oh,' Jimmy wagged his head in characteristic fashion, 'it was the week you got Bill I think. Aye, about that time, because he remembered you telling me to tell the man to keep the change. You said, "What's sixpence." I saw him at it through the window the first time, but I thought I was mistaken until the next time he came in an' I watched him.'

'But why didn't you tell me, Jimmy?' Corny's voice had risen now.

'Aw, boss, ask yourself. Anyway, I tried twice but both times you were in a bit of a stew about something and I thought I'd better not make matters worse.'

'You know what you are, Jimmy, you're a fool, that's what you are, you're a long, lanky fool!' Corny was shouting now. 'I've known this money's been going all the time, but I thought it was you.'

'Aye.' Jimmy jerked his head. 'I know that.'

'Well, you didn't think I was so green as not to miss pound notes and ten shilling notes going out of the till, did you?'

'Well, you didn't say nowt, boss. Anyway,' he now hunched his shoulders up, 'I couldn't give him away; he sort of, well likes me and trails after me. Aw, I just couldn't, so I thought it was better to clear out an' you find out for yourself. But then, well he brings me the tin and tells me he's done it for me so's I won't go.'

'Oh, my God!' Corny sat down heavily on the stool and, leaning his elbow on the desk, he supported his head. He'd go barmy. After a moment he looked at Jimmy and said, 'You know I don't want you to go, don't you?'

'I don't want to go either boss.'

'You've got fixed up at Baxter's.'

'Aye, I start on Monday.'

'Could you back out?'

Jimmy looked down towards his boots, then said, 'Aye, I could, but then you've got the other fellow startin' Monday.'

'Oh, that can be fixed,' said Corny. 'We've said for some time we could do with another hand. And he's young and I won't have time to see to him myself and train him. How about it?'

148

'Suits me, boss.' Jimmy was grinning slightly, and Corny got off the stool and went towards him and again he said, 'You're a fool, Jimmy. No matter who it is—now you listen to me, man, woman or child—don't you take the rap for anybody, not for a thing like that, for stealing.' He drew in a long breath, then putting his hand out and gripping Jimmy's shoulder he said, 'Nevertheless, thanks. And I won't forget you for this. Now where is he?'

'I set him cleaning a rod in the shed. You won't come down too hard on him, will you?'

'You leave it to me. This one lesson he's got to learn and the hard way.'

As Jimmy walked quickly by Corny's side he asked, under his breath, 'Where's Mrs. Boyle?'

For answer Corny said, 'It'll be all over by the time she gets downstairs.'

David stopped rubbing the rod as soon as he caught sight of his father. Jimmy wasn't there, there was just his dad, and when he saw the look on his face he began to tremble.

'So you've been stealing from me?' Corny was towering over him.

'N . . . not pro . . . proper stealing, Dad.' It was as if he had gone back six months and was learning to pronounce his words again.

'There's only one form of stealing. If you take something that doesn't belong to you that's stealing, proper stealing.'

'I . . . I d-didn't want J-J-Jimmy to go, D-Dad.'

'Jimmy could have asked me for the money. If Jimmy had wanted a share in that car he could have got the money. He didn't want you to steal for him.'

'You said it di-didn't matter, Dad.'

'What didn't matter?'

'Mo-money.'

Corny remembered faintly saying, 'What's money for but to go round.'

'You knew it mattered, didn't you? If it didn't matter why did you do it on the sly? Why did you go to the office when I wasn't there and take money out of the till if it didn't matter? You knew it was stealing. You wouldn't go upstairs and open

149

your mother's purse and take money out, would you?'

David was past answering. He was staring at Corny, his eyes stretched to their limit.

'Take your pants down.'

'N-n-no, Dad, P-please, Dad.'

'You'll take your pants down, or I will.'

'M-Mam!'

'Your mother isn't here and if she was that wouldn't stop me from braying you. Come on.' He made a grab at him and in a second he had pulled the short trousers down over David's hips, but even before he had swung him round and over his knee David had started to holla, and when Corny's hand descended on his buttocks for the first time he let out a high piercing scream.

Ten times Corny's hand contacted his son's buttocks and it must have been around the sixth ear-splitting scream that Rose Mary entered the drive.

She knew that noise, she knew who cried like that. She ran to the garage and was borne in the direction of the hullabaloo, and she was just rushing through the small door when she saw her mother coming from the yard. She was running like mad towards the repair shed.

'Corny! what are you doing? Leave him go!'

When Mary Ann went to grab her son from her husband's hands he thrust her aside, and as he stood David on his feet he cried at her, 'Now don't start until you know what it's all about.'

'I don't care what it's all about; there's no need to murder him.'

'I wasn't murdering him, I was twanking his backside. And he's lucky to get off with just that. Do you know what he's been doing?'

Mary Ann said nothing, she just stared at her son. His face was scarlet and awash with tears, and from his face she looked to his thin bare legs and the side of his buttocks that outdid his face in colour.

'He's been stealing. This is the one that's been taking the money from the till, and all the while I thought it was Jimmy.'

Mary Ann couldn't speak for a moment, then she whispered,

'Oh, no! Oh, no!'

'Oh, yes.'

'David! you couldn't.'

Now David did a very strange thing. He did not run to his mother where he knew he would find comfort, but he turned to the man who had been thrashing him, and laying his head against his waist he put his arms around his hips and choked as he spluttered, 'Oh! Oh! Oh! Dad.'

Corny swallowed deeply, wet his lips, then bending down he pulled up the trousers and fastened them round his son's waist.

Rose Mary had been standing at her mother's side, absolutely too shocked to utter a word. Their mam smacked their bottoms sometimes, but ... but she had never seen anybody get smacked like her dad had smacked David. He said David had stolen money. Eeh! it was a lie because David never did anything without telling her. He would not even steal without telling her. But then David wouldn't steal; he knew it was a sin, and he'd have to go to confession and tell Father Carey. Their dad was awful. She didn't love their dad. Poor, poor David. Her feelings now lifted her in a jump to her brother's side, and David did another surprising thing. With the flat of one hand he pushed her away, and whether it was with surprise or whether she tripped over one of the jutting pieces of wood that supported the engine on the bench, she fell backwards. And now she let out a howl.

She howled until she reached the kitchen and Mary Ann, taking her by the shoulders, shook her gently, saying, 'Now stop it. You weren't hurt; stop it, I tell you.'

'He ... he pushed me, our David pushed me.'

'He didn't mean to, he was upset.'

'Dad said he stole. He's tellin' lies, isn't he?'

'If your dad said he stole, then he stole. And that's what he's been thrashed for. Now go to the bathroom and don't pester him or question him because he's upset. Run the bath for me.'

'Have ... have we to go to bed, Mam?'

'No, I'm just going to give David a bath, then he'll feel better.' She did not add, 'It might ease the pain of his bottom.'

As Rose Mary went slowly out of the kitchen Corny came in and stood near the table, but he didn't look at Mary Ann as he gave her the explanation for David stealing the money. When he had finished there was a pause, and then she said, 'You'll have to make it up to Jimmy somehow.'

'Yes, yes, I intend to.'

He now said, 'I can't understand how he could do it under my nose.'

Mary Ann went into the scullery and put the kettle on the gas and she stood near the stove for a moment and turned her face towards the kitchen door. She wanted to shout out, 'It shouldn't surprise you; anybody could have walked off with the garage these past few weeks and I doubt if you would have noticed.' But of course she didn't. That was over, over and done with; except that the corpse was still lying between them and nothing would be the same again until it was removed. And the only way to remove such a corpse was to talk about it, and that was going to be very difficult for them both.

CHAPTER FIFTEEN

PATTERNS OF LIFE

'It's a wonder you're not struck down dead, Rose Mary Boyle. Eeh! I just don't know how you can. Like me mam says, if you got paid for being a liar you'd own the world.'

'I'm not a liar, Annabel Morton, and I'm not like you, thank goodness; I'm not a common, ignorant, big-mouthed pig!'

'No, of course, you're not, you're a common, ignorant big-mouthed idiot, that's what you are.'

'What is this?' The cool voice of Miss Plum brought Annabel Morton round to face their teacher, and Miss Plum raised her head and said, 'School hasn't begun yet and you've started.'

Rose Mary warmed suddenly to her teacher. 'She's always on, Miss Plum, she never lets up. She's always at me and our David, isn't she, David?'

David made no response. He was still in a way suffering from the effect of Friday, having his ears boxed by Diana Blenkinsop, then being thrashed almost within an inch of his life, at least that's what Rose Mary had told him had happened. But in any case the effects of the thrashing had caused him to be sick on Saturday, really sick; nervous tummy, his mam had called it. Then on Sunday his Grannie McMullen had come. She had heard about him trying to cut somebody's hair off. His grannie heard everything; she was the devil's mam, their Rose Mary said, and he could believe it. She hadn't heard about the money he had taken, and for that at least he was thankful. But she had heard about all the money his mam was getting because Ben had died. She had wanted to know what his mam was going to do with it and his mam had said they were going to have a bungalow built at the bottom of the field.

If he had known his mother was going to get all that money he would never have taken any from the till because yesterday she had given Jimmy the money he wanted for his share in the car.

The money was making things exciting and he felt he was missing a lot having to come to school; and here was Miss Plum at them already. Well, if she wasn't at them she soon would be; he could tell by the look on her face and the way she had shut up their Rose Mary.

And Miss Plum had shut up Rose Mary, she had shut her up with one word, 'ENOUGH!' Then after a pause she turned to Annabel Morton and said, 'You are not to call people liars, Annabel.'

'Yes, Miss Plum,' said Annabel meekly, before adding, 'But she is, Miss Plum. Do you know what she said? She said her mam's been left a fortune an' she's going to build a bungalow and going to give their house to Jimmy, who works in the garage. And she said her mother's a writer and she gets lots of money from the *Newcastle Courier...*'

'Well, she does, you! She does.' Rose Mary was poking her chin out at the unbelieving individual.

'That's enough.' Miss Plum's voice was stern now, 'And Annabel is quite right this time, you are lying, and you've got to...'

Miss Plum was utterly amazed as Rose Mary slapped at her skirt and dared to say, 'You! you're as bad as she is. It's true ... 'tis!'

'Don't do that!' Miss Plum had caught the hand and slapped it twice. 'You're a naughty girl, Rose Mary; I'll take you to the ... Oooh!'

Miss Plum couldn't believe it was happening. Only the pain in her shin where David's hard toecap had kicked her proved to her that it had happened. Rose Mary Boyle had slapped at her and David Boyle had kicked her. 'Well!' She seemed to swell to twice her height and twice her breadth. As her hands went out to descend on them they turned and fled.

David was now racing across the school yard in and out of the children with Rose Mary hanging on to his hand, but just

154

as they reached the gate he pulled her to a skidding stop. And there he turned and looked at the sea of faces mostly on his eye level, except the enraged countenance of Miss Plum. And it was to her he shouted one word, 'HELL!'

Then running again, almost flying, they scampered up the road and they didn't seem to draw breath until they reached the bus stop, and there Rose Mary, gasping, stared at her brother, at their David, who had sworn a terrible word at Miss Plum. She, herself, had slapped at Miss Plum's dress but their David had kicked Miss Plum, he had kicked her on the shin and made her yell; and then he had said that word.

Quite suddenly the enormity of this crime and its penalty, of which she would be called upon to share, was too much for her and she burst out crying.

David stood looking at her helplessly. He didn't feel at all repentant, at least not yet. After a moment he said, 'Here's the bus.'

She was still crying as they boarded the bus. It was their nice conductor and he said, 'Hello. What's up with you two? It isn't ten minutes ago I dropped you. This day's flashed by.'

They didn't answer, and when they were seated he came up to them and, bending down, said, 'What's happened this time?' And Rose Mary, sniffing and gulping, said, 'She called me a liar, Annabel Morton, and the teacher came and she took her part and ... and I said, I wasn't a liar and I put my hand out, like that.' She tapped the conductor's coat. 'And she slapped my hand.' She paused and cast a glance at David, but David was looking down at his finger nail as it intently cleaned its opposite number, and raising her face further to the conductor she whispered, 'He kicked her.'

'He did!' The conductor's voice was laden with awe. 'Go on.'

Rose Mary closed her eyes and nodded her head and went to impart something even worse, placing her mouth near his ear, she whispered, 'He swore.'

He brought his face fully round to hers, trying to shut the laughter out of it by stretching his eyes and keeping his lips firm; then he said, 'He swore, did he?' Now his mouth was

155

near her ear. 'What did he say?'

'. . . Hell.'

'HELL!' The conductor straightened up and cast a glance at the interested passengers around them, and his look warned them not to titter.

'By! He's done it now, hasn't he?' The conductor looked at David's bowed head. 'Once upon a time he never opened his mouth, did he? And now, by, he's not only opened it, he's using it, isn't he?' He was talking as if David wasn't there, and Rose Mary nodded at him, then said, 'We'll get wrong.'

'Oh, I wouldn't worry.' The conductor jerked his head now.

'But we will; we'll be taken to the priest.' She turned her head swiftly to look at the man behind her who had made a funny noise, but the man's face was straight.

'What do you think he'll give you?'

'Who?'

'The priest, when you're taken to him?'

'Likely a whole decade of the Rosary, I usually only get one Our Father and three Hail Marys.'

Now the conductor turned abruptly away, saying, 'Fares, please. Fares, please,' as he went down the bus.

He was a long time down the bus because everybody was talking to him, and some people were laughing. Rose Mary thought she would never laugh again.

When they stood on the platform waiting for the bus to stop the conductor put his hand on David's head and said, 'You'll do, young 'un, you'll do,' and David grinned weakly at him. He felt he stood well in the conductor's estimation. For a moment he wished the bus conductor was his dad, at least for the next hour or so.

When they entered the lane Rose Mary started crying again, and once more he took hold of her hand, a thing he hadn't done, except when he pulled her out of the school yard, for a long, long time.

When they came in sight of the garage he drew her to a stop and they stared at each other. Rose Mary was frightened. He was frightened, but he wasn't crying. When she said to him, 'We'll get wrong,' he made no reply, and they walked on again.

156

It had never entered their heads to run anywhere else but home.

When Mary Ann, having made the bed and tidied the room, went to adjust the curtains she imagined she was seeing things when she saw them hand in hand walking slowly across the drive towards the front door. She pressed her face near the window for a moment; then she turned and flew down the stairs, and as she opened the door Corny was approaching them from the garage, and they both asked the same thing in different ways: 'What's the matter? Why have you come home?'

'Mi ... Miss Plum, Mam.'

'Miss Plum! What's she done?'

'She wouldn't believe us.'

Mary Ann bent down towards Rose Mary. 'She wouldn't believe you? What did you tell her?'

'About everything in the school yard. Annabel Morton called me a liar, and a pig, and then she told Miss Plum what I'd said and Miss Plum said I was lying an' all. And I didn't mean to slap her, Mam, I didn't; I just touched her skirt like that.' She flicked at her mother's hand now. 'And she slapped me, she slapped me twice. And then David....' She turned and looked at her brother, but David was looking up at Corny, staring up at him, fear in his eyes again, and Corny said, 'Yes, well? What did David do?'

Rose Mary waited for David to go on with the tale, but David remained mute and she said, 'He only did it because she slapped me, Mam, that's why.'

'All right, all right,' said Mary Ann patiently, 'but tell me what he did.'

'He ... he kicked her, and he said ...'

'You kicked, Miss Plum?' Mary Ann was confronting her son, and David looked at her unblinking but said nothing.

'How could you, David.'

'He only did it because she was hitting me, Mam.'

Mary Ann took in a deep breath and Corny let out a slow one, and then Mary Ann asked of her daughter, 'What else did he do?'

Rose Mary's head drooped slightly to the side, her eyes

157

filled with tears again, she blinked and gulped but couldn't bring herself to repeat the terrible thing their David had said to Miss Plum, and so Corny, looking at his son, asked him quietly, 'What else did you do, David?' And David looked back at his father and said briefly, 'Swore.'

Corny moved his tongue round his mouth as if he were trying to erase a substance that was sticking to his teeth, and then he asked, 'What did you say?'

There was quite a pause before David said, 'Hell!'

'. . . Hell?'

'Uh-huh!'

'Why?' Corny felt he had to pursue this, and seriously, but David went mute again, and Rose Mary, now that the worst was over, quickly took up the story. 'He grabbed me by the hand and pulled me away from Miss Plum and it was as we were going through the gate he turned back and he shouted it at her.'

Both Corny and Mary Ann saw the scene vividly in their minds, and simultaneously they turned away and Mary Ann said, 'Come along, come upstairs.'

They had hardly entered the room when the phone rang and, Corny picking it up, said, 'Yes?' and Jimmy answered. 'It's the schoolmistress. She wants to know are the bairns back.'

'Put her on.' Corny now looked at Mary Ann and she reached out and took the phone from him; then with her other hand she waved the children out of the room, whispering, 'Go into the sitting-room, I'll be there in a minute.'

'Mrs. Boyle?'

'Yes, this is Mrs. Boyle.'

'Have the children returned home?'

'Yes, they've just got in, Miss Swatland.' Mary Ann's voice was stiff.

'I suppose they've given you their version of the incident?'

'Yes, Miss Swatland.'

'They were very naughty you know, Mrs. Boyle. Of course, being twins it's understandable that they'll defend each other, but in this case they were very, very naughty. Do you know that David kicked Miss Plum?'

'I understand that he did.'

'And that Rose Mary slapped her?'

'I don't think Rose Mary slapped her. She made a movement with her hand at her skirt; there's quite a difference.'

There was a short silence on the line now, then Miss Swatland said, 'Rose Mary has a vivid imagination, Mrs. Boyle. This isn't a bad thing unless it gets out of hand and then there's a very thin line between imagination and lies.'

'Rose Mary wasn't telling lies, Miss Swatland.'

There was a gentle laugh on the other end of the line 'Oh, Mrs. Boyle you don't know what Rose Mary says at school, what she said today. I understand she said you had come into a fortune, and you were giving your garage boy your house and building a bungalow, besides which you were writing for *The Courier*, and on and on.'

'Which are all true, Miss Swatland.'

There was a longer pause now, and the sound of whispering came to Mary Ann and she glanced at Corny and inclined her head towards him.

Miss Swatland was speaking again. 'Well, you must admit, Mrs. Boyle, such things don't happen in the usual course of events, and when a child relates them one is apt to think they are exaggerating, to say the least. Miss Plum wasn't to know of your good fortune.'

'Miss Plum could have thought there may have been some truth in the child's prattle. It isn't unheard of for people to win the pools, is it, although I haven't won the pools. And I think when a child is using her imagination, even when there isn't any truth as a basis, it doesn't help her to be told she is a liar.'

'Miss Plum has a lot of small children to cope with, Mrs. Boyle. . . .'

'I'm quite well aware of that. Well, she'll have two less in the future, Miss Swatland, because I'm going to take the children away.'

'Oh, that is up to you, Mrs. Boyle.'

'Yes, it's up to me, Miss Swatland. Good day.'

'Good day, Mrs. Boyle.'

Mary Ann put the phone down and looked up at Corny, and

Corny said, 'Take them away? But where will you send them?'

'Her to the Convent, and him to St. Joseph's Preparatory.'

As he turned away from her and walked towards the window she said quietly, 'We can do it between us.' Then going swiftly to the sideboard drawer, she took from her bag an envelope and went to his side and handed it to him, saying, 'That's for you. You won't be able to actually get the money until it goes through probate, but it's just to let you know that it's yours.'

'What is it?'

'Open it and see.'

He looked at her a full minute before he did as she bade him, then when he saw the solicitor's letter he bit on his lip and handed it back to her, saying, 'I can't take it.'

'Corny! Look at me.'

He looked at her.

'We . . . we've always shared everything and I won't spend another penny of the money unless you take half. I mean it. That's go to straight into your personal account when it comes through. It's not going into the business, it's for you to do as you like with. I don't want you to put any of it towards the bungalow, and I won't, that's to come out of the business. You always intended to build a house, didn't you?'

He had his head bowed deep on his chest and he said, 'Mary Ann.'

She didn't answer him, she waited, but he seemed incapable of going on. When she saw his jaw bones working and the knuckles shining white through his clenched fists she turned away and said, 'What about us going down to Fanny's this afternoon. We've never been for ages.'

It was still a while before he answered, and then he said briefly, 'Aye.'

'The . . . the children would love it, and there's something I want to give her.'

Again she went to her bag and took out another envelope, and as she looked at it she said, 'It's wonderful to be able to do things you've dreamed about.'

He half turned his head towards her, his eyes still cast

down, and she looked towards him and said, 'It's fifty pounds. They gave me an advance. Oh, I'm dying to see her face when she ...'

'Oh, God!'

She watched him swing himself round from the window and go to the chair by the fireside and, dropping into it, bury his face in his hands, and when he muttered thickly, 'Coals of fire,' she could say nothing, only stand by the table and press her hands flat on it and look down on them and wait.

Corny squeezed his face between his hard palms. She was going to give his grannie fifty pounds. Nobody, not one of her ten sons and daughters she had alive, or any of her offspring, had ever given her fifty shillings, except perhaps himself—he had always seen to his grannie—but Mary Ann was going to give her fifty pounds; only she would have thought about giving her fifty pounds; only she would have thought about saying I'll not spend a penny of my money unless you take half. And he had been such a blind and bloody fool that he had let his thoughts and feelings slide from her. For weeks now there had been superimposed on her a pair of long, brown legs and a face that he had thought beautiful. In this moment he couldn't imagine what had possessed him not to see through the slut the moment he clapped eyes on her, but the point was he hadn't. Instead some part of him had gone down before her like dry grass before a fire.

For days now he had been consumed with shame, yet he kept telling himself that nothing had happened, not really. He hadn't been with her, he hadn't kissed her, he hadn't even touched her. That was funny. He had never once touched her hand, yet he was feeling as guilty as if he had gone the whole hog, and he knew why, oh aye, he knew why, because deep in his heart he had wanted to. Mary Ann had sensed this and nothing would be right between them until he could tell her, until he could own up.

'Mary ... Mary Ann.'

'Yes.'

'I'm ... Oh, God, Mary Ann, I'm sorry.' He gazed up at her, his voice low and thick. 'Oh, God, Mary Ann, I am, I am. To the very heart of me I'm sorry. As long as I live I'll never

161

hurt you again.' His eyes were tightly closed now, screwed deep into their sockets, and when her arms went round him and he pulled her on to his knee, she held his head tightly against her and for a moment she couldn't believe that the shaking of his body was caused by his crying. Corny crying. She had first met him when she was seven and he had been in her life since and she had never known him to cry.

The tears were raining from her own eyes now, dropping down her cheeks and on to his hair, and she moved her face in it and tried to stop him talking. Some of his words she couldn't catch, they were so thick and broken and mumbled, but others she picked out and hugged to her heart, such as 'Nothing happened, nothing, ever. Believe me, believe me—never touched her—not her hand. Like madness—As long as I live I swear to you I'll never hurt you again ... never in that way. Oh, Mary Ann. Why? Why? Why?'

'It's all right, it's all right.' She held his head more tightly and rocked him as she repeated, 'It's all right. It's all over now, it's all right,' and while she rocked him she thought of the time just before she got married when her da had become fascinated by that young girl, and after she herself had exposed the girl for what she was her da had struck her, and then he had gone out into the night and the storm, and her mother had thought he had gone for good, but in the early dawn Michael had found him in the barn, exhausted and her mother had taken the lantern and gone to him. It was odd, she thought, how patterns of life were repeated.

CHAPTER SIXTEEN

FANNY

The children bounced on the back seat of the chair chanting, 'Great ... gran ... Mac ... Bride's!' and each time they bounced Bill fell against one or the other, until he felt forced to protest.

Mary Ann, screwing up her face against his howling, turned round and, dragging him up, hoisted him over the seat on to her knee.

'Ah, Mam, he was all right.'

Mary Ann looked over her shoulder at Rose Mary and said, 'He sounded all right, didn't he? A little more of that and he would have been sick.'

Bill settled down quietly on her knee, and the children took up their chant again, and Corny drove in silence. He felt washed out, drained, but quiet inside. The turmoil had gone.

Mary Ann, too, felt quiet inside, spent. She had to talk to the children but all the while her mind was on other things. She thought in a way it was a good thing they were going to Fanny's. Life became normal when in Fanny's company.

Most of the Jarrow that they passed through wasn't familiar any longer. New blocks of flats, new squares, new roads; soon even Burton Street and Mulhattan's Hall would be gone. As a child she had longed to get away from the poverty of this district, from the meanness of Burton Street and the cramping quarters of Mulhattan's Hall where there were five two-roomed flats and privacy was a thing you could only dream of. Yet now, as the car drew towards the house, she thought, Once they pull it down that'll be the end of Jarrow—at least for me. And, what was more serious, once they pulled it down it certainly would be the end of Jarrow for the Hall's oldest occupant.

Fanny spied them from the window and she was at the door to greet them in her characteristic fashion.

'In the name of God, has your place been burned down! It's no use coming here for lodgings, I can't put you up ... Hello, me bairns. Good God Almighty! what's this you've brought?' She pointed to the dog and Rose Mary shouted, 'Can't you see, Great-gran, it's a dog.'

'It's Bill. I told you about him, Great-gran,' said David. 'You know.'

Fanny bent towards David and, digging him in the chest with her finger, said, 'Aye, you told me about a dog, but you wouldn't call him a dog, would you? Snakes alive! I've never seen anything so ugly in me life. Get your things off, get your things off all of you, the kettle's on. How are you, lass?' She bent and kissed Mary Ann. Then looking at her grandson, she said, 'It's no use askin' you how you are, you're never anythin' but all right.' She paused now and added, 'There's always a first time. What's the matter with you? Have you got a cold?'

Corny stretched his face and rubbed at his eyes, saying, 'Yes, I've got a bit of a snifter.'

'It looks like it an' all. Well, you keep it to yourself, I don't want any of of it. Well, sit yourselves down, can't you. Go on.'

When they were all seated she looked from one to the other and said, 'You might have given me a bit of warnin', to descend on me like this. You're not exactly manna from heaven, an' I haven't a thing in for tea.'

'Well, if you don't want us we can go.'

She took her hand and pushed at Corny's head. 'You'll go soon enough if I have any of your old buck.'

'How you keeping, Fanny?' Mary Ann now asked, and Fanny, lowering her flabby body down on to a straight-backed chair, said, 'Aw, well, lass, you know by rights I should be dead. Sometimes I think I am and they've forgotten to screw me down. Look, what's he up to, sniffing over there?' She pointed to Bill who was investigating beneath the bed in the far corner of the room.

'It's likely the last two months' washing attracting his attention,' said Corny.

'Mind it, you. I don't put me dirty washing under the bed.' She nodded straight-faced at him. 'All my dirty washing goes on the line, outside.'

They were all laughing together now and Mary Ann thought, Oh, it's good to be with Fanny.

'And what have me bonnie bairns been doin'?' Fanny embraced the two standing before her, and Rose Mary, laughing up at her, said, 'Oh, lots and lots, Great-gran.'

'Such as what?'

Oh. Rose Mary looked at David, then glanced back at her mother, and when she finally looked at Fanny again she was nipping her lower lip, and Fanny said, 'Oh, it's like that, is it?'

'It's like that,' said Mary Ann. 'We won't go into it now, it's too painful.'

'Aw.' Fanny nodded her head while she cast a glance down on the averted eyes of her great-grandson, and, bending down to him, she whispered, 'What you been up to this time, young fellow me lad? You murdered somebody?'

When David's head began to swing and his lips to work one against the other, Mary Ann put in, 'I might as well tell you. They both ran away from school this morning.'

'You're jokin'!'

'I'm not joking, Fanny; they're both very wicked. You won't believe what I'm going to tell you, but Rose Mary there slapped her teacher, and David, well he not only kicked her in the shins but swore at her. Now I bet you won't believe that of your great-grandchildren.'

Fanny, dropping her gaze to the two lowered heads, said, 'Never in this wide world, I wouldn't believe it if the Lord himself came down and said, "Fanny McBride, if you don't take my word for it you'll go to hell".'

Rose Mary's head came up with a jerk. 'That's what he said, Great-gran. It's true, it is, it's true. He did, he said that word to Miss Plum.'

'Hell? Never!'

'He did, didn't you, David?'

165

There was pride in Rose Mary's tone now, and Fanny, pulling herself to her feet and pressing her forearm over her great sagging breasts, turned away, saying, 'This is too much. It's the biggest surprise of me life. I'm away to get the cups, I must have a sup tea to get over that shock ... Mary Ann, can you help me a minute?'

Mary Ann reached the scullery just seconds after Fanny and found her standing near the shallow stone sink over which there was no tap. Fanny motioned her to close the door. Then her body shaking all over, she gave way to her laughter, and Mary Ann, standing close to her, laughed with her.

'He told her to go to hell?'

'As far as I can gather.'

'And he kicked her shins?'

'Yes, oh yes. The headmistress was on the phone a minute or so after they got in.'

'He's a lad; he's going to be a handful.'

'You're telling me, Fanny.'

Fanny dried her eyes; then patting Mary Ann on the cheek she said, 'Aw, it's good to see you, lass. I had the blues this mornin'. You know, I get them every now and again, but they were of a very dark hue the day, and I lay thinkin', Tuesday, what'm I gona do with meself all day. But I said a little prayer and left it to Him, and here you all are, lass. But tell me,' she bent her face close to Mary Ann, 'is everything all right?'

There was a pause before Mary Ann said, 'Yes, Fanny.'

'There's been somethin' up, hasn't there?'

Mary Ann now lowered her head and said in a whisper, 'Yes, Fanny.'

'I knew it. When he popped in last week-end there was somethin' about him. It's gone now. I looked at his face when he came in at the door and I knew it was gone. But he's been in trouble, hasn't he?'

Mary Ann turned her face away as she said, 'You could call it that, Fanny.'

'Money?'

'Oh, no, Fanny.'

'Not the business then?' Fanny's eyebrows moved upwards.

'No.'

There was a longer pause before Fanny whispered, 'You're not tellin' me that my Corny would ever look at . . .'

'Fanny.' Mary Ann gripped the old woman's hands. 'I'll pop in some time towards the week-end, when I'm down for my shopping, and tell you about it, eh?'

Fanny's head moved stiffly and she said, 'Aye, lass, do that, do that.' Then, turning to the rack where the cups hung, she asked in a louder tone, 'What brought you down the day anyway?'

Now her tone lighter and louder, Mary Ann answered, 'Well, we wanted to see you.'

'I'm flattered I'm sure, but is that all? I've never seen the gang of you on a Tuesday afore in me life.'

'I had a present for you and I wanted to give it to you myself.'

Fanny turned round with four cups in her hand and she said, 'A present for me? Well now; why do you have to bring me a present on a Tuesday afternoon, it isn't me birthday? And it's neither a feast, fast, or day of obligation as far as I can gather, and it's weeks off Christmas. Why a present?'

'Must there be a reason why I want to give you a present?' Mary Ann poked her face at Fanny across the table. 'I just want to give you a present, that's all. Here, give me those.' She took the cups from Fanny's hands and placed them on the saucers on the tray, and as she did so she said, 'You could do with some new ones.'

'Aye, I could that. Those that aren't cracked or chipped haven't a handle to support them. Aw, but what does it matter? Go on, I want to see this present you've brought me.'

She stopped just within the kitchen and, nodding towards Bill where he lay on the floor by the side of the bed, she said, 'I'm glad of one thing, it's not him.'

As she went to the hob to lift up the teapot that was for ever stewing there she said, 'Well, come on, where's that present.' And when she turned round, the teapot in her hand, Mary Ann handed her the envelope.

Fanny put the teapot on the table, then with her two hands she felt all round the envelope, and the thickness of it, and she looked at Mary Ann, then at Corny, and from him to the

167

children, and they all looked at her, waiting for her reactions.

'Well, go on, open it.' Mary Ann could have been back twelve years in the past, bringing her friend a present on her birthday, or at Christmas, and saying to her, 'Well go on, open it!'

Fanny put her finger under the flap but had some difficulty in splitting open the long brown envelope, and when at last the jagged edges sprang apart she stared at the money.

Slowly she withdrew the notes. They were five pound notes and were held together by an elastic band, and her mouth dropped into a huge gape as she flicked the edge of them one after the other. They appeared to her as a never-ending stream. She lifted her eyes and looked at Mary Ann. Her expression didn't show pleasure, and you couldn't say she looked surprised, not just surprised; amazed, yes. She now looked at Corny and said, 'What is this?' Then, her eyes blinking a little and the suspicion of a smile reaching her lips, she said, 'You won the pools?'

'No.' Corny shook his head. 'Mary Ann's come into some money.'

Fanny now looked at Mary Ann again and she said, 'You've come into money, lass? From where?'

'You remember Ben, Fanny, you know who used to look after Mr. Lord.'

'Aye.'

'Well, he died, and ... and he left me nearly all his money, over eight thousand pounds.'

'Eight thousand pounds!' It was only a whisper from Fanny now, and Corny, sensing the flood of emotion that was rising in his grannie, hoped to check it by saying, 'Aye, and she's throwing it about right, left and centre; she's thrown half of it my way.'

'Half of it?' Fanny turned her attention to Corny now, but her eyes seemed glazed and out of focus. 'Well, aye, that's understandable. But me. All this?'

'It isn't that much, Fanny, it's only fifty pounds.' Mary Ann's voice was soft, and Fanny now looked at her and her lips trembled before she brought out, 'Fifty you say? Only fifty pounds. Lass, do you realise that I've never had fifty pounds in me hand in me life afore. I've ... I've never seen fifty pounds all at once in me life afore. And ... and what am I going to do with it?'

'Light the fire with it if you like, Fanny,' Mary Ann was smiling gently.

Fanny put the envelope down on to the table and, turning from them, her shoulders hunched, she went towards the scullery again, only to be stopped by Corny saying, 'Come on now, none of that.'

A moment ago Fanny's body had been shaking with laughter, now it was shaking with her sobbing.

When Corny sat her down in her chair, Mary Ann put her arms around her shoulders and, her own voice near tears too, she said, 'Oh, Fanny, look. I wanted to make you happy, not to see you bubble. Come on now, come on.'

But the more Mary Ann persuaded, the more Fanny cried, difficult, hard crying, crying that was wrenched up from far below her brusque, jocular, life hardened exterior.

Now the children were standing at her knees, Rose Mary with the tears running down her face and David with his tongue probing one cheek after the other in an effort not to join her.

While this was all going on Bill had been lying quietly enough on the old clippie mat by the side of Fanny's bed. He liked this room. There were smells here quite different from those at home; there was a spice about the smells here that reminded him of the morning he had met that girl, the one who had led him to the grab, and of the one solitary lamp-post he had yet encountered.

From under the bed there was wafted to him at the present moment the musty, stingy, yet bracing aroma that had attracted him as soon as he entered the room. They had said he hadn't to go near it, but it was drawing him, inching him towards it. He turned one fishy eye in the direction of his people. They were all gathered round a chair, nobody was looking at him. The smell said, 'Come on; it's now or never.' And so, without rising, he wriggled forward and there it was, the source of this delight. It was soft and deep and warm. He pushed his nose into it. It gave him a tickly feeling that urged him to play, so he took a mouthful of it and shook it. But when it fell over his head he didn't care much for that, so he wriggled to get from under it, but the more he wriggled the more it enfolded him. This was too much of a good thing. If he didn't do something about it he'd be smothered, so, biting and scrambling, he fought until he was free.

He had reached the other side of the bed and brought the thing with him. He was in the open now, and knew how to deal with it. The smell was more exciting in the open, it was sending shivers all over him. When he saw all the feathers floating about him he growled his delight, and dashing round the bed he dragged the old eiderdown with him.

'Look. Look what he's got, Dad. Bill!'

'Oh, godfathers! Here, you rattlesnake you, give that to me.'

'Don't pull it, Corny, don't pull it, it'll only make him worse.'

'In the name of God! how did he get hold of that.'

'You shouldn't leave such things under the bed.' Corny was yelling at Fanny now, and she, getting to her feet, flapped her hands here and there to ward off the rain of feathers.

'Corny! Corny, I'm telling you, don't pull it. I'll get him. Leave it, just leave it; you're making him worse. And you let go, David.'

Bill had never had such a game in his life. He growled his delight; he knew the more he pulled the more feathers he could raise; and his people were enjoying it too. Like all his breed he loved to give pleasure to humans, if not to his own species, so he pulled and he pulled.

'Let me get behind him.' Mary Ann was yelling at the top of her voice. 'Leave go, Rose Mary. Are you all mad? Do you hear me, the lot of you! Don't pull it!'

When at last it got through to the children and Corny that they were only adding havoc to chaos, Bill had sole possession of the tattered eiderdown again and they could hardly see each other through the cloud of feathers.

They drew the down up their nostrils then sneezed it out. When they opened their mouths to speak they swallowed feathers. They were all spluttering and coughing and flapping

170

their hands as if they were warding off a swarm of bees.

After sneezing violently, Mary Ann cried, 'Leave ... leave him to me. Now, now just keep quiet and leave him to me.' Then she moved slowly towards Bill who was at the far side of the table, quiet now, stretched out to his full length with his front paws lying on the edge of the eiderdown and his blunt snout resting between them.

'Bill. Bill darling. Go ... od boy. Give it to mother. That's a go-od boy. Bestest boy in the worldie world.' She was almost crooning as she approached him, and Bill looked at her lovingly. Here was his best pal, here was the one he liked best of the lot. Here was someone who understood him, who talked with him and played with him when the others weren't around. Well now he would give her a game like she had never had before.

When he up and dashed from her, dragging the eiderdown with him, she threw herself full length on it, and the result was disastrous. Pulled to an abrupt stop his never very steady legs gave way and he overbalanced and landed against Fanny's feet, and in the process of scrambling up again he dashed between them, and over she went.

Corny was standing within a yard of her, and springing forward he grabbed at her as she fell, hoping to break her fall; and luckily he did. It was also lucky for him that the old chair was behind him and he found himself almost pushed through the sagging bottom of it with Fanny's weight on top of him.

There was a moment of utter silence in the room; then it was broken by a rumble of laughter, a rumble that could only erupt from a chest as deep as Fanny's.

Corny, from his cramped, contorted position, had the wind knocked out of him, but the shaking body of his grannie raised in him a chuckle, then a laugh, then a roar. And now Rose Mary and David, each tugging at Fanny's hands, joined in with a high squealing glee.

And Mary Ann?

Mary Ann was lying on the eiderdown, her face buried in the crook of her elbow. When she raised her head it was to look into the eyes of Bill, who was prone once more, his muzzle flat out, staring at her. She now looked about her, at

171

the shambles the room represented, then ceilingwards, at the feathers floating and settling everywhere, then she looked at the huddle of her family in and around the battered armchair, and she joined her voice to theirs. She laughed and laughed until she felt that if she didn't stop she'd be ill. But it was cathartic laughter; it was what they needed to dispel the last of the nightmare. And it could never have come about except at Fanny's. Oh, thank God for Fanny.... And Bill. Oh, yes. She put out her hand towards Bill and he wriggled his body forward. Oh yes, and Bill.

The Mary Ann stories

A GRAND MAN
Filmed as 'Jacqueline'
'Mrs Cookson's Geordie humour never lets her down.'
—Michael Swan, *The Sunday Times*

'The character drawing is excellent, Mary Ann herself is a real joy and one senses the truth of the background.'
—*The Times Literary Supplement*

THE LORD AND MARY ANN
'A completely successful sequel ... It is a continuation of the adventures of Mary Ann Shaughnessy, a child of the Tyneside ... so good.'—John Betjeman, *The Daily Telegraph*

THE DEVIL AND MARY ANN
'Mary Ann is sent to a "posh" boarding school in Sussex to learn how to become a lady ... Warm, cheerful, family stuff.'
—*Books and Bookmen*

LOVE AND MARY ANN
'The people are real and not only Mary Ann is vital ... The author knows the locality and the people she writes about.'
—*Vanity Fair*

LIFE AND MARY ANN
'The Tyneside heroine of this series is now a teenager, with the troubled spirit that she showed as a child. Family reading: a joy.'
—*Books and Bookmen*

MARRIAGE AND MARY ANN
'As, with a sudden mist before our eyes, we prepare to follow Mary Ann up the aisle, we realise Mrs. Cookson has lost none of her magical touch.'—Marjorie Bentley, *Shields Gazette*

MARY ANN'S ANGELS
'Mary Ann now has six-year-old twins, who cause her heart-

aches as well as happiness.... Although Mary Ann may grow older, she remains as endearing as ever.'—*Guardian-Journal*

Each of the first five *Mary Ann* books had been read as a serial on *B.B.C. Woman's Hour.*

THE INVITATION *by* CATHERINE COOKSON

When the Gallachers received an invitation from the Duke of Moorshire to attend his musical evening, Maggie was overwhelmed. Naturally, she did not see the invitation as the rock on which she was to perish; nor was she prepared for the reactions of her family. Her son Paul, daughter Elizabeth and daughter-in-law Arlette were as delighted as she was but the effect on Sam, Arlette's husband, was to bring his smouldering hate of his mother to flashpoint. Maggie herself, however, was to be prime mover of the downfall of the family she loved too dearly . . .

0 552 09035 2—35p   T59

OUR KATE *by* CATHERINE COOKSON

An Autobiography

The *Our Kate* of the title is not Catherine Cookson, but her mother, around whom the autobiography revolves. She is presented with all her faults, yet despite these, Kate comes out as a warm and lovable human figure. And against this central character, we see the child Catherine going to 'the pawn', fetching the beer, and collecting driftwood from the river—for the family struggle through an era when work was scarce and social security non-existent.

So *Our Kate* is a story of a person and a period. It is an honest statement about living with hardship and poverty, seen through the eyes of a highly sensitive child and woman whose zest for life and unquenchable sense of humour won through to make Catherine Cookson the warm, engaging and *human* writer she is today.

0 552 09373 4—35p   T60

A SELECTED LIST OF FINE NOVELS
THAT APPEAR IN CORGI

All these books are available at your bookshop or newsagent: or can be ordered direct from the publisher. Just tick the titles you want and fill in the form below.

CORGI BOOKS, Cash Sales Department, P.O. Box 11, Falmouth, Cornwall.
Please send cheque or postal order, no currency, and allow 10p to cover the cost of postage and packing (plus 5p. each for additional copies).

NAME ....

ADDRESS ....

(MAY 74) OP3